The Opiate

Your literary dose.

"There's no use in denying it: this has been a bad week. I've started drinking my own urine."

-Bret Easton Ellis, *American Psycho*

"And while I wait/I put on my perfume/Yeah I want it all over you/I'm gonna mark my territory."

-Britney Spears, "Perfume"

Editor-in-Chief
Genna Rivieccio

Editor-at-Large
Malik Crumpler

Editorial Advisor
Anton Bonnici

Contributing Writers:

Fiction:

Poetry:

Criticism:

Editor's Note

Pissing. I think about it a lot. Not in the sexual way most golden shower-loving men would want you to, but in the way that examines how much it can actually limit you from being able to function in an "average" day-to-day life. Or rather, what a merciless capitalist society *wants* people to view as average. This, for most, still tragically means enduring the eight-hour workday in a five-day workweek. Try as Robert Grosse did to convince the suits of implementing otherwise in his 2018 book, *The Four-Day Workweek* (a tome presently very hard to come by at an affordable price, which seems telling of the fact that the corporate overlords don't want their labor slaves to get any funny ideas...as if people get their ideas from books anymore).

At the same time, *They* say it's important to drink the advised amount of water every day. At present, that means roughly three liters for men and two liters for women. Those who actually adhere to that guideline (and I am someone who does) will find that they are frequently bound by an invisible string that leads straight to the nearest *toilette*. Begging the question: how is one supposed to work a conventional full-time job *and* engage in the much touted practice of self-care? Hell, even bare minimum care. It seems like one of those impossible-to-answer riddles that can't actually be answered because, ultimately, you're just supposed to "figure it out." "Make it work." Even if that means sacrificing your health to partake of the "required hours." The ones that still, no matter what you do, can't quite translate into enough money to pay for all that you need to, let alone any of the "extras" you might foolishly desire.

And it *is* foolish to desire (sometimes synonymous with hope), because it always sets you up for disappointment. But that very cycle is what the system in place is founded on. And what it banks on. So that, every time you might tell yourself you can be free of it, it reels you back in (and no, please do not make *The Godfather* [*Part III*, no less] correlation, "Just when I thought I was out, they pull me back in"). This not only extends to working a thankless, underpaid job that expects you'll magically finagle a way to piss on your own time (even if you're drinking the recommended daily amount), but also to the notion—especially for women—that one must "find a mate" in order to continue this vicious, never-ending (not until human extinction anyway) circle. The circle of capitalism, not life.

As discussed frequently in the era during which it's less and less chic to revere capitalism (mainly because fewer people than ever are benefiting from it), many are well-aware by now that the system reinforces the social construct of monogamy. And it is, despite what we have for so long been conditioned to believe, just that: a construct. Merely another key aspect of the propaganda we see all around us every day, which tells us that monogamy is quite simply "innate." Built into our DNA, our primordial nature. Complete with an internal mantra that chants, "Find, attach and propagate" (and yeah, for many animals, that means pissing somewhere to mark territory and "allure"). But what would it mean for society at large if this cycle were to be broken? If women themselves could stop being so preprogrammed to attract men, to be "appealing" to them. And by "appealing," what is meant, of course, is *visual* appeal. Not mental. For, try as blokes might to insist they just love a woman who can "think for herself," the fact of the matter remains that most conventional straight men would prefer a woman who effectively amounts to a blow-up doll: easy on the eyes and doesn't say too much. Or if she does, let her words please just parrot his own thoughts and "philosophies."

Yet, despite being aware of this and having it reiterated on a daily basis (purely via the evidence provided by the people who run governments), women can't seem to let go of the idea that they need to somehow be pleasing to men. And always apologize when they "fail" at that task. As men themselves would if they were put in the same position. In truth, men fail far more at pleasing women than the other way around. Women just happen to be more forgiving about it. But that's starting to change. Forgiveness, in the end, isn't all it's cracked up to be (just look at Jesus).

And so, one has to keep dreaming of what women might be further capable of if they weren't still so bogged down and imprisoned by the notion of "being beautiful." Of constantly worrying about "attracting." How liberating it would be to relinquish such mind- and potential-draining concerns. As it would be to drink as much water as you needed (and even wanted) to throughout the day without getting anxiety about how using the bathroom might automatically brand you as a "weak" member of the pack. An inferior worker bee (I realize I just mixed animal and insect metaphors, but whatever). All because you dared to stop and tend to your needs as a result of tending to a larger need before that: thorough hydration. But society as we currently know it is designed in such a manner that actually taking meaningful measures for optimal survival—an act designed to strengthen us—is the very thing that makes us "feeble" in a typical work scenario. Or rather, "defective" on the assembly line pace of capitalism.

On my way to the *toilette* regardless,

Genna Rivieccio
January 16, 2023

P.S. Gray wolves are (mostly) monogamous, but it feels more genuine and true because they aren't doing it largely out of financial convenience.

FICTION

Black Market Encounters

Danila Botha

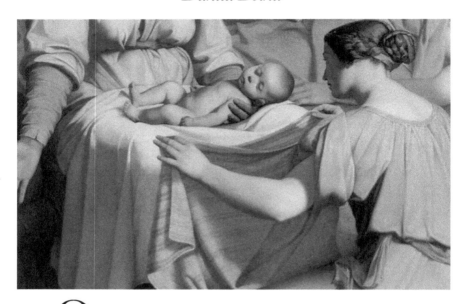

Officially, our group is called Black Market Encounters: Finding Love in Unexpected Places. Once, our psychiatrist jokingly called us the Meet-Brute Club; another time, the Dead Wives Club. We're a support group for people who met their partners in unconventional ways...when they weren't single but were deeply unhappy. People generally have a low threshold for hearing about these kinds of socially unacceptable relationships—unless it's to champion the poor, aggrieved wife. Most of us had gotten tired of lying. It's not even that we cared what other people thought, we just wanted normal things. Friends, people who understood us and didn't judge.

This is where Dr. Marcus Black came in. He found us online, through a survey. He even pays us to be here. That's how important we are to his research, he says. He provides us with snacks and drinks, crackers and brie, sugar-free candy and wine and, as he puts it, "A safe place to air our grievances and connect with others who've engaged in similar patterns of behavior."

We would meet once a week in his office, with its soft carpeting and multiple plush leather sofas. In the past, most of us might have laughed at the idea of needing a safe space, but Dr. Black's voice was so warm and comforting, and having him sit there, taking notes, telling us that what we thought or felt made sense *and* was understandable, well, that seemed like such a balm. The truth didn't set us free exactly, but it gave us back a bit of our former selves. I can't tell you how liberating it's been, realizing that I can be around people who know the truth, but still like me. I've made new friends, and my husband, Andrew, thinks that's great, which is really something, because he's totally anti-therapy.

I met Andrew through my job. Let me elaborate: I'm a midwife, and I met him when I was helping to deliver his and his then wife's baby.

Andrew and I lived in the same neighborhood, we frequented the same artisanal doughnut shops, the same pet store (we're both cat people) and the same liquor store. We could have met reaching for the same organic salmon treats for the cats we were each fostering, for the same cat rescue downtown. Even if we were low on money, we both spoiled every cat as if they were our own.

I'd been a doula for five years before I decided to become licensed as a midwife. When I met Andrew, I was almost fully certified, but I was still assisting the main midwife on call. He wasn't often there, and when he was, he was visibly anxious, fiddling with his pale fingers, and pacing back and forth. I registered his piercing blue eyes, and his sandy blonde hair. It seemed strange that someone so uncomfortable in his own skin would remind of me of family vacations at the beach.

You meet two types of husbands as a midwife. There's the kind who breathes heavily and tells you that *he* would be the one carrying the baby himself if he could. And he sweats, holding his wife's hand, doing breathing exercises, complaining that he's exhausted. As if what he's doing is the same as what she's doing.

Then there's the hands-off kind. The ones who volunteer to take care of the other kids, or run every possible errand. If they *are* there, they're reading books or articles, asking questions that imply that they know more than us, that what we do pales in comparison to Dr. Google.

Andrew wasn't trying to prove how devoted he was, and he wasn't condescending towards us either. He was terrified.

I wasn't surprised when he told me that the baby hadn't been planned. He'd never wanted to have kids, and Angie, who'd played it cool, and never said so outright, always did. He'd asked her to marry him, he said, after four years of dating, because even though she claimed she didn't care, she was getting restless. Every person in his life told him what a catch she was.

The name Angelina suited her. She was a red-haired beauty in the Pre-Raphaelite sense, with pale skin and a gap between her front teeth that kept her from looking *too* perfect. Angelina also once told me she was proof that perennially sarcastic women could still land great husbands.

Her birth plan included blasting "Under Pressure" by Queen and David Bowie, followed by "Fruits of My Labor" by Lucinda Williams if it was going well or "The Drugs Don't Work" by The Verve if it wasn't. Still, she couldn't hide the unadulterated joy that snuck into her eyes as she got closer to giving birth. Occasionally, excitement overtook him too, but he always whispered it to me, not her. Suzanna,

> "We're a support group for people who met their partners in unconventional ways...when they weren't single but were deeply unhappy. People generally have a low threshold for hearing about these kinds of socially unacceptable relationships..."

the more experienced midwife, looked at me oddly when I told her what I'd observed.

"Why do you care so much? Let's just focus on the baby," she insisted.

I tried to support Angie, but she shrugged me off, quipping, "It's good that there's two of you. Andrew needs a babysitter."

What do you do when a woman practically throws her husband at you at the exact moment when they should be bonding? As per her request, I spent most of my time with him. It was her first pregnancy, so it went on for twenty-seven hours, and we had time to sit in their kitchen, drinking terrible coffee. We talked and talked. When his daughter was born, Angelina told me her name was Allegra because she made her so happy. And distracted. That's why Andrew motioned for me to follow him into the backyard. We stood next to the red plastic baby swing he'd put up. It was too dark to see any stars. He leaned me against the brick wall, careful not to set off their motion detector, and kissed me. I looked up and the moon hung above us like a thin sliver of hope. We'd been awake for almost forty-eight hours and everything felt like a dream. I looked down at my wrinkled green scrubs, felt my hair bursting out of its ponytail. I was fifteen years younger than him. When Angie went back to work after a month, I joined him to babysit whenever I could. He took six months of paternity leave. I'm a hundred percent sure I spent more time with Allegra than she did.

Andrew was a better father than either of us expected. When Allegra napped, and she napped *a lot* (for three to four hours at a time), Andrew and I made love...and then made plans for the future. I didn't really believe it until he told her he was leaving her for me. Allegra had just turned one. Angie lost her shit, crying and screaming, eyeliner smeared like an emo kid from the 2000s. But after we got married, and now that I'm pregnant, she's calmed down a little. She still refuses to call me Allegra's stepmom. I started getting more emotional in my second trimester, which is when I found Dr. Black. It's such a relief to just admit how much I wanted him. I do feel guilty, if I let myself think about it. So I try not to. How can you feel bad about something if it ended up leading you to everything you always wanted? Maybe Andrew and I were just meant to be. My closest friend in the group is Alexis. One night, Andrew and her boyfriend, Cole, bonded in the parking lot when they were both waiting to pick us up, and we all started hanging out. Alexis is angular, with long, shiny brown hair, meticulously tweezed eyebrows and a heart-shaped face. She has a perfect, placid smile for the other women in our group, and a wicked half-smirk for me when she's making fun of them afterward.

Like me, she had a job that required her to care for other people. She worked one-on-one with autistic kids, assessing their needs and progress. Cole was the father of one of her clients. She'd never seen such a dedicated, hands-on dad, she told me. She'd mostly always dealt with the moms.

"I couldn't pick his ex out of a lineup," Alexis remarked. "I literally never saw her. Cole came to get Jesse every single day. He wanted to talk about him in so much depth. He'd call me and want to hear about everything. Jesse is such a smart and sweet boy, we really bonded and, after a while, he even told me that he loved me. Cole looked so exhausted every time I saw him, because the kid was always up all night, and *he* was the one staying up with him."

It happened gradually, she explained. She or Cole would text each other just to say hi. She found after-school programs for Jesse, and celebrated with Cole when they went well. Their first kiss was in the parking lot, while they were waiting for another therapist to bring Jesse outside. They had sex in the backseat of his car a few days later. He told her that he hadn't had sex in two years. Not long after, he left his wife for Alexis and she started working at a different support center. Also like me, his ex-wife hates her. What bothered Alexis the most was that she said that Alexis had all the sensitivity of a robot, but this was based on only having met her twice.

Alexis found out about Dr. Black through her friend, Kaylee, who was a former nanny to the stars. The dad was a famous hockey player, and the mom was a singer and actress. She was one of three nannies for their two kids. The wife hired her, and they got along great. She took her shopping, gifted her with her old designer handbags and jewelry and overpaid her. One day, she led her to their giant walk-in closet, gave her a twenty-four-karat gold dildo, dropped her pants and showed her how to use it. Soon, they were having sex regularly, and when her husband came back, they had their first threesome. They called her their sex toy, and it happened a few more times until they fired her with a generous severance package and a seven-page-long NDA.

There was Kathleen the teacher, who'd slept with several teenage boys. Kathleen had confessed through her lawyer and had a very short prison sentence. It was hard to imagine her in jail. She had perfect posture, wavy brown hair and green eyes that she hid behind rimless, nerdy glasses. She looked and acted older than twenty-five. She didn't like our jokes, made faces when we swore and refused to drink with us. The boy was sixteen and lived with his aunt and uncle. His mom died when was he was very young. He wore a Beatles t-shirt to class one day, and they connected. "He's an old soul," she said. His name was Avi. The fact that they were still in touch was something we all swore we'd never repeat to anyone.

There were other less interesting stories. Like the daycare owner who fell in love with a married mom, who left her wife for her. Or the marriage counselor who slept with some of the husbands, but insisted they stay in their marriages.

The person everyone talked about most was Kendra. She'd sit near the edge of the room, fidgeting with her hair and her phone. Kendra used to be an oncology nurse in the best cancer unit in the city. Her job was her life's work, but everything changed when she met Isabella and Darion. Isabella was only twenty-eight and had stage three lymphoma. She was beautiful and in shape, a first-grade teacher who ran half-marathons for charity every year. Her room was always full of balloons, stuffed animals and cards signed in messy crayons by eager, uncertain little hands. When she met Darion, she fell hard. He had sleek, wavy hair, a generous smile and gentle eyes. He called himself a children's rights advocate instead of a family lawyer. He liked to bake. He'd drop off cookies that he'd make every day at the nurse's station. She loved his traditional coconut drops, a family recipe that he said took him back to his childhood with every bite. Kendra was

"In the past, most of us would have laughed at the idea of needing a safe space, but his voice was so warm and comforting, and having him sit there, taking notes, telling us that what we thought or felt made sense *and* was understandable, well, that seemed like such a balm."

supposed to tell him that Isabella was getting incrementally better, but she didn't. She pumped Isabella full of antihistamines (and lots of tramadol) to make her drowsy during the day. She told her it was for the pain, but that only added to Isabella's confusion. She gave her an anesthetic to knock her out all night. Sometimes, Isabella barely recognized Darion. Kendra told him to prepare himself for the worst. Darion and Kendra used to meet after her shifts and walk around the parking lot together. One early morning, they held hands and he gripped her so hard her knuckles turned white. Isabella, in one of her few lucid moments had told him that if she didn't make it, she wanted him to move on and marry someone he could have kids with.

Darion kissed Kendra and ran his fingers through her hair for the first time. Kendra started canceling shifts to spend more of her precious hours with him. One day, a colleague of hers dropped in at

. apartment to see Kendra and caught them together. Isabella eventually got better. Darion never talked to Kendra again and she lost her job *and* her license.

On what was supposed to be our last session, Dr. Black dressed more formally, showing up in a suit instead of his usual jeans and white polo shirt.

He passed out a questionnaire. It started out with us ranking ourselves from zero to three based on statements about loyalty and empathy, relationships and our current partners. Then there were questions about our ambitions, and how we saw ourselves. We filled them in obligingly. He looked our answers over in front of us, thanking the group for cooperating and helping him with his research. He'd use pseudonyms, he assured, but we were to be his featured "anecdotes." He asked us how we characterized ourselves, and someone raised her hand and said, "Determined." There was a murmur of approval, and someone else said that we were fearless romantics. Alexis declared we were brave and unapologetic.

"*I* think," Kendra added in her slow, slightly paranoid cadence, "that you were studying us to see if we had some kind of disorder."

People started shifting uncomfortably.

Dr. Black confirmed it and quietly told us what this had really been about, but I could barely hear him over my own anger and the sound of scraping chairs and jackets zipping up.

"I can't believe this," I heard someone saying, over and over.

Kathleen stood up and threw her bag down. "You've been telling us that what we feel is okay. What the fuck did we trust you for? How could you do this to us?"

"My dear, there are certain people who won't admit who they are, even to themselves. They certainly wouldn't participate in a trial like this. But I needed access. No one ever admits to having these disorders. And once you out people, they run away..."

"We should sue you..." Kaylee snapped. "I have some experience with lawsuits now."

"We should all go on Rate My MD and give you zero stars. We should tell everyone how deceptive and awful you are..." someone else chimed in.

"Ladies, these conditions are spectrums, so if you believe what I've observed to be true, it's a question of severity." He stated the words gently, but they were a cold comfort.

He tried to get us to go over and talk to him, so he could tell us if we were overt or covert, malignant or antagonistic. Did we want to know where on the scale we all stood, he asked, and we ignored him.

He tapped on my shoulder so gently I hardly felt it. "Aurora, you actually ranked lower than I originally expected."

I let his previous diagnoses sink in. *Narcissistic Personality Disorder. Antisocial Personality Disorder. Sociopath.*

I glared at him, willing him to feel guilty. He just shrugged back.

"I feel deceived," I finally said.

He grinned creepily. "Not so great when the shoe is on the other foot, is it?"

As I stood outside with Alexis, her hands shaking while she tried to light her cigarette, we heard Kendra come up behind us.

"Can you believe this guy?" she seethed, and we shook our heads.

She leaned in so close we could smell her sandalwood rose perfume.

"Don't worry," she whispered. "I've got enough drugs left to make this the Dead Shrink Club. If not, I know some people who can help us."

We stared at her black puffy coat until she disappeared into the night.

Sexageddon

Alex Encomienda

At Club Bonneville, 12:30 a.m.

Sheridan walked up to the bar after carefully eyeing the scene. There were smug women huddled in groups, men jumping up and down in a state of reckless ecstasy at the center of the dance floor and plenty of people dressed in provocative clubwear. The orgiastic crowd was oozing sexual energy, but not everyone was going to leave with "a score."

When the bartender approached, Sheridan demanded, "Let me get a shot of whiskey and a can of Red Bull."

As he was waiting for his drinks, he saw a woman who looked vulnerable. In *his* mind, she was perfect. She looked attractive enough to have sex with, and yet carried an aura of insecurity. She might be considered generally *un*attractive to most men, but he knew that he had a fondness for those kinds of women. She looked *real*.

Sheridan had done this several times before. He picked some- one up and went home a "lucky guy." He thought, if nothing else, he could at least get a taste of what she was like. So he sidled up to her and announced, "Hi, I'm Sheridan. Is this seat taken?"

Turning shyly, she replied, "No, go ahead."

"I see a fine woman sitting by herself and I have to ask, are you single? By the way, what's your name?"

She smiled. "I'm single, and I'm quite happy that way. I know most of the guys here are looking for someone to hook up with, but I'm not that kind of girl. And the name is Ella."

"Well, perhaps we can just talk and get to know each other,

"Did you know that a woman can have an orgasm so strong, she can trick the physiological reaction into a constant surge of prolactin which will make her orgasm for several hours straight? Yeah, just when you might have thought women got the raw end of Darwin's deal, God throws you a puzzle box."

Ella. I can assure you, I'd be worth your while. If we end up hitting it off, maybe we can even make out. No harm in that, right?"

She arched her brow. "I just told you, I don't do that stuff. I'm here to have a good time. I've never put out before traditionally dating someone and I won't start now. I only have sex with someone I'm in a serious relationship with. I'm not like the other women here. If that's what you're after, find someone else."

At that moment, the bartender finally gave Sheridan his drinks. He took the shot of whiskey and then chased it with the Red Bull.

"Oh yeah, that was good," he exclaimed as he caught her looking at him.

"How can you drink whiskey like that? It's disgusting."

"You'd be surprised. As a matter of fact, human beings are a fascinating species. Did you know that, theoretically, a human can consume twenty ounces of vodka and not be drunk in the slightest? It's all a matter of *how* you drink it. Same goes with sex. Did you know that a woman can have an orgasm so strong, she can trick the physiological reaction into a constant surge of prolactin which will make her orgasm for several hours straight? Yeah, just when you might have thought women got the raw end of Darwin's deal, God throws you a puzzle box."

Ella balked at the idea. "That's bullshit."

"Well, believe it or not, it happens. Wanna find out for yourself?"

She smirked. "Does this kind of talk usually get you laid?"

"Not gonna lie, it's helped me before."

She paused. He noticed a glint in her eye that wasn't there before as she asked, "What are you, like, a scientist or something?"

"Well, I'm more of a philosopher...but I don't believe in pseudointelligence. And don't get me started on cod philosophy either. I simply take things from life that make sense to me and use them as a tool to shape myself. All of life is much more complex than we give it credit for."

She nodded along. "Well, that's awesome. I really hope you find what you're looking for."

Sheridan bit his lip, still hoping for more. "Do you want to go to a park or something? Perhaps take a walk? It's getting kind of stifling in here."

She gave him a blank stare and then, out of nowhere, conceded. "Okay. Sure."

At Miranda Gentry Park, 2:15 a.m.

Sheridan let his head fall back while keeping his left arm on the steering wheel. Ella was sitting next to him. Both were observing the train station across the street from the empty lot where he had parked. They watched the trains pass by as he continued to elaborate on the philosophy of sex. The concept behind the Pareto principle came up, and he went on about eugenics and the art of being a Chadlite.

"Do you know what you need in your life, Ella? You need someone who won't bullshit you and knows what he wants right away. You need the raw, unfiltered closeness of being passionate and intimate with someone for the sake of acknowledging your own mortality. Or maybe, the bottom line is, you just need to get *fucked* really hard."

He slowly reached over and put his hand on her thigh. "Kiss me. We don't have to do anything else, Ella. I can trust that we'll both go home satisfied if we share this one kiss."

She raised her head slightly and he saw her eyes glistening from the reflection of the street lights. He knew that, even though he wouldn't get to have her completely, he could be satisfied with just the taste of her lips, and feeling them push against his.

He could go home with that. If not for the instant, carnal gratification, then for the benefit of his ego and self-esteem.

As he was staring deeply into her eyes, he saw her reach below her waist. To his delighted shock, Ella then hurried to pull up her skirt and remove her underwear. "I want it, Sheridan. Give it to me. Pound me, Sheridan!"

Although in a state of awe and disbelief (and rightfully so), Sheridan proceeded to remove his clothes and eagerly lifted up the middle armrest so that he could lay her down and get on top of her. He felt her bare skin against his chest and smelled her warm, sweet breath as it filled his nostrils. However, something was wrong. He touched himself and he realized that he was still limp. He did not understand his lack of a physical response, because he was clearly aroused.

Confusion.

"Is something wrong?" she asked.

In a state of panic and humiliation, desperate to say anything, he uttered, "I-I'm sorry, I don't know what happened. I'm just nervous, that's all. Did you want to give me your number and we can do this another night?"

Ella hurried to put her clothes back on and abruptly left his car, slamming the door behind her.

There was quietness, and then the blaring horn of an incoming train from afar.

Redemption

Laurence Klavan

"Horse trading," "pony up," "two-horse race"—so many of the old timer's expressions were equine. Was this the way he saw himself, as sub or unhuman? Or maybe Kingston was just lathering on the country boy routine as thick as his white head of hair (his "thatch" of hair was a better way to put it) because it was more rural, more Huck Finn, or however the hayseed saw himself.

Could Kingston actually *be* this stupid, Crater wondered? He was a senator, after all. Of course, that could just mean he was cunning, ruthless and obnoxious. Crater bet Kingston hadn't read half as much as *he* had in jail, where he'd finally gotten into reading (he'd barely cracked a spine—a book's spine, that is—as a boy).

If you had told Crater when he *was* a kid—or an adult, for that matter—that one day he'd be sitting opposite and negotiating with an old Southern senator, he would have said *get outta here*...or just kicked you in the ass. That was simply the kind of miscreant he had been. But Crater had committed no major crimes, just mischief (another old-hat word, like "thatch"). Your standard-issue petty larceny, pickpocketing, shoplifting and the like. Road rage, of all things, was what had landed Crater in jail. That was the funny part; he'd gotten away with all the rest. He'd been penalized for impatience, really. For selfishness and im- maturity, because he couldn't stand to be stuck in traffic a minute longer and had exited his vehicle to tell the guy one car ahead of him just that. Then he bashed the poor sap's window in before trying to stand and dance on his hood, soon after sliding off it since the surface was too slick (and Crater too drunk) to stay upright. It hadn't been the other guy's fault; he'd been stuck, too, and was actually being adult about it. Unlike Crater, who, at long last, had gotten what he deserved by being forced to (at longer last) grow up.

His sentence had been to serve weekend jail time, plus community service—picking up trash in a park—and seeing a social worker. Her name was Ramona, and she took an immediate liking to him. (Not the same way Crater took a liking though, fantasizing about her because she was a fine, maybe fifty-year-old and he wasn't that much younger/also open-minded about age—anyway, forget it, she couldn't have cared less about him in that way...preferred women, it turned out). Liked him enough, in fact, to put his name in for the program, the new one begun by the government.

And Crater had been chosen, that was the amazing thing. They'd read his application and decided he deserved it. The whole idea of the program was to give guys like him—selfish, incorrigible fuck-ups—a chance to have the responsibility, authority and dignity they'd long been denied. To "expand the pool," as they put it, of who could be leaders in the country. In short, to give a sorry excuse of a person like Crater some power...at least briefly.

Crater was shocked by the happy look on Ramona's face when she heard. Who'd *ever* been happy for him? His mother, father, ex-wife? Nobody. For the first time, he felt proud. It was a new emotion, almost better than any drug he'd taken or sex he'd had. It made Crater want to do a good job in the position he'd been granted, a better job than he'd ever done at anything.

President of the United States, after all, was a big deal. Crater would only be president for a week while the actual president "rested." Crater himself had never voted and wasn't registered (he didn't think)—couldn't remember and hadn't checked. Because, honestly, what would have been the point for a guy like him? The week it happened was, by good or bad luck, budget negotiation time, and temporary President Crater had decided to do it personally. Not leave it to some boring old budget director, as everyone assumed he would. That's how he came to be across the table now from corny and hirsute (a jail word) Senator Kingston. He was an infuriating fellow in the actual president's party or the other party, Crater couldn't remember, considered a "tough customer" and "hard nut to crack." (Crater had dismissed the "working group," a subpar crowd of earnest and boring people, to go mano a

23.

mano with him). Kingston was still at it, the old annoyance. Was it to show he was a gambler, a daredevil? Someone who would "go the distance" (another horse expression...or was it boxing?) for his "needy constituents," as he called them. Of course, Crater knew they weren't "constituents" so much as high rollers, big contributors, fat cats. That's who Kingston wanted the dough to trickle down

"Could Kingston actually *be* this stupid, Crater wondered? He was a senator, after all. Of course, that could just mean he was cunning, ruthless and obnoxious. Crater bet Kingston hadn't read half as much as *he* had in jail, where he'd finally gotten into reading (he'd barely cracked a spine—a book's spine, that is—as a boy)."

to, because that's where it always went in this country: pushed into the pockets, stuffed down the bras and spilled on the palms of the privileged. It was always a windfall for the wealthy, a stipend for the selfish for the rest of their lousy lives!

Well, not under seven-day President Crater, it wouldn't be. Now that *he'd* been given the gig, he found religion—not real religion, of course...*that* bored him senseless. But rather, Crater wanted to enact a "payback," a "redistribution of wealth," as it were, to compensate for this country's crimes and his own stupid life of not caring about anybody besides himself.

Senator Kingston didn't believe he was sincere, thought there was a catch. That Crater had an angle. Corrupt people couldn't comprehend that not everyone was like them, their cynicism a way to avoid truly seeing themselves, absolve themselves of their own latent guilt. But finally, Kingston agreed to Crater's demands because he bet that, in the end, the funds would be flung at those who didn't really need them, that Crater was as big a crook as him—right? As they parted ways, the senator even slapped the back of his new pal, Mr. President-for-a-Week.

***

Months later, Crater wondered what Kingston would have said after seeing the government's gift finally being distributed, going where it would do the most good. He waited, anxious to witness the look on the recipient's face.

He knew she wouldn't be as a little as the last time he saw her, which was a few years earlier (he couldn't remember how many). He wasn't thinking straight or being responsible then. When she showed up, Crater saw that his daughter, June, looked very different at her now six years of age. His ex-wife had dropped her off and driven away in a mad flurry, yelling, "Have her back at five—and don't be your usual awful, selfish self!"

Then Crater watched as June was diverted from staring at him—slightly scared, for he was a virtual stranger—to what he and the government had bought for her. Crater got the idea while haggling with Kingston, and it had been quite a stroke of genius, if he did say so himself.

The pony had a big blue bow around her neck, like the great gift she was. She'd come as a special delivery from Saudi, the finest mare in the world. It would make up for all his years of neglect. *Who was the selfish one now*, Crater wanted to demand of his ex.

"Daddy!" June cried, thrilled. After hugging it and hugging it, she said, "I can't wait to show my friends. Can they ride her, too, Daddy? Can they?"

The new statesman and benefactor pondered the request for a moment. Then, growing into the change in his life, he replied "No. *That* would be wrong."

Antediluvian

Charles Holdefer

Paul had never forgiven him. And now, a phone call out of the blue.

It came while his son, Milo, was displaying his mental prowess. He announced that he'd memorized the periodic table of the elements, handing his father a photocopy so he could prove it.

"Okay, go," Paul said.

Milo began to recite. "Hydrogen, helium, lithium, beryllium..." He reeled off the first fifty correctly before he hesitated, his face clouding. "Osmium?"

Paul shook his head. "You skipped a couple. Take your time."

Milo clenched his jaw and squinched his eyes. Paul could almost hear a crackle of synapses. "Iridium?"

"No, sorry."

Milo squeezed his fists to his temples—and then Paul's phone rang.

"Gaaah!" His son threw out his arms.

"But that was impressive," Paul insisted, ignoring the repeated ring. "You got most of them."

"Leave me alone!" Milo stomped out of the room.

Paul answered his phone.

"Did you see? We're on the news!"

No, he certainly wasn't expecting this call. For the last twenty-two years, he'd avoided speaking to this man. When Bobby identified himself, Paul was momentarily at a loss. He blinked at the periodic table.

"What news?"

"Local—channel seven. They found our drawing in Carson Cave. It's a sensation! This might be our best stunt yet."

"Huh? I don't have anything to say to you. How did you get my number?"

"Bobby's tone, the assumed complicity—it was like a door had opened onto a lost world. As if they were still kids, playing pranks and laughing till their sides hurt."

"Come on, Doctor Big Shot. Whether you like me or not, we'd better figure out how to handle this. We need a strategy."

"I don't know who 'we' is."

"I'll send you a link."

***

Years ago, to celebrate victory in a high school baseball game, they'd gone to Carson Cave to drink beer. Bobby had stolen a cooler. His technique was brazen, targeting an unattended picnic table when its occupant was distracted by a child near the boat dock. Bobby swooped in, grabbed the cooler and exited without breaking a stride. The operation took three or four seconds. Then, avoiding the road, he descended on a footpath to the river.

"Timing," he shrugged, popping a beer. "That's all it is."

Paul nervously kept watch on the path, near the mouth of the cave. Bobby claimed to have discovered the place himself, though Paul didn't believe him. At sunset, the light angled into the entrance and gave the stone a golden glow. The mouth of the cave wasn't visible from the path, but they kept their voices low. Bobby had thrown down a pair of sleeping bags to make it comfortable. He called it Carson Cave because his last name was Carson and he wanted to take credit.

Tonight, they were in the grip of a buzz, even before they started drinking. Paul had pitched a hard-fought game and Bobby, playing second base, had contributed two hits. It was impossible to go home before they'd processed their victory and analyzed its twists and turns. Not everyone appreciated why this was necessary. Paul's parents assumed he would win, while Bobby's parents had no time for trivial things like baseball. They stayed home to care for his sister.

"I'd like to live here," Bobby mused, admiring his cave. "If I could hook up a TV, I would."

Paul laughed. His friend still indulged in little boy fantasies, and he wasn't embarrassed to admit it. Maybe Bobby half-believed his words.

Bobby picked up a rock and scratched on the wall. "Look at you, man." A crude figure emerged, its arm flung back. At first, Paul assumed it was a depiction of himself, pitching, but Bobby kept scratching and the arm grew longer, thicker: it was a bat.

Next he sketched another figure, a woman of exaggerated voluptuousness, her arm extended. She was the pitcher.

As a final touch, he added an oversized penis to the batter.

"You and Frances," Bobby explained.

"Jesus, Bobby. That's just stupid. Grow up."

"Think you can do a better job?"

Before the light faded, Bobby sketched in extra touches and details—a campfire, an orb sailing in the air. He worked fast, accidentally discovering that another rock, moistened with spilled beer, allowed him to add red highlights. Paul found a similar stone and helped out, embellishing his figure, making himself taller. The drawing acquired a goofy charm as they became immersed, acting on each other's suggestions.

Then it got too dark and they finished a twelve-pack, listening to the river.

***

The link Bobby sent included a story about the discovery of

ancient cave paintings near the Reed River. Authorities had been alerted and the site was sealed off. A paleontologist at the local university said it was evidence of a prehistoric community in the area. "This will oblige us to rethink our timeline and our understanding of migration patterns."

Good Lord, Paul thought. *Is there anything people* won't *swallow?*

He didn't bother to return Bobby's call, but the next day, when Paul was double-parked outside Monaco's Deli and waiting for his wife, Sandra, Bobby called again. "Did you check out the link?"

"Yeah, I saw it."

"You haven't told anyone, have you?"

"Why should I tell anyone? They'll put two and two together. I suspect the old beer cans are a pretty good clue."

"I never left any. I needed the deposit. Listen, Paul, I got a plan—"

"And I don't want to hear it."

Sandra had stepped out of the deli with their takeout order. Monaco's was overpriced, but he and Sandra had put in a long day at Owl Optics and didn't feel like cooking. He shut off his phone. Sandra slid into her seat, smelling of tomato and basil. They drove on to pick up Milo from his guitar lesson.

***

Back in the cave, he'd been in love with Frances Talucci. He hadn't told a soul, but Bobby had sniffed it out. In those days, Frances attended an all-girl Catholic school and was a star pitcher in fastpitch softball. Ordinarily, their paths wouldn't have crossed...except one day, during a rain delay, teams playing parallel tournaments at the city park found themselves biding time at a gymnasium. Pitchers were throwing to keep warm. His eyes lingered on a stocky girl, high-busted, with long, curly hair and a wicked underhand delivery. *Smack*. Her velocity was impressive. *Smack*. Others gathered to watch and soon a challenge emerged. "Anyone want to face her in the batting cage?"

No one stepped forward. Sure, Paul's teammates laughed and feigned indifference, but there was a tension in the air, and the reason was obvious. Nobody wanted to get shown up by a girl. *Smack*. Everybody stood around, waiting for someone else to react. So Paul selected a bat and stepped forward.

She walked up to her mark and gave him a little nod. He nodded back.

A pause, then her arm whipped. He swung and fouled it backward. Barely got a piece of it. Her unfamiliar motion put him off balance.

He felt the gaze of his teammates, how much they were rooting for him, and suddenly the pressure felt greater than in a real game, because this wasn't a game: he was representing the guys.

He jumped on the next pitch too early and the ball trickled harmlessly to his left, another foul.

Now she took longer to set up. He was aware of his body, his

"Remember those guys in England with crop circles? If we're smart, we could play it like that, only bigger. The question is, when is the time to come forward and take credit? How do we capital- ize?"

hunched stance, his exposed, bony wrists. Frances looked at her glove where she gripped the ball, concentrating, then she lifted her eyes, searching for the right spot. Her arm whipped.

He swung and missed completely.

A few hoots and whistles—oh sure, none of it was serious, was it? Just fooling around in the gym. He gave her a quick wave and replaced his bat in the rack. He went back to resume his throwing, acting very busy.

Soon, word came that the weather had cleared and they could go outside again. Everyone gathered up their kit bags. He looked in her direction. She was heading for the door. Then she saw him.

Again, she nodded.

Years later, Paul replayed this moment countless times in his mind, but he couldn't remember what he did next, whether he acknowledged her sign. He was a blank. But she walked straight toward him. "Can I talk to you for a minute?"

Paul didn't move. Was she going to gloat?

"Thanks for stepping up," she said.

He laughed nervously. "Not my finest moment."

"I wouldn't say that. None of those other guys were brave enough."

She smiled as if they shared an understanding, and then she walked on. Paul wished he'd said something clever. He was unable to shake the image of her brown eyes and thick hair, her smile, and the jut of her hip as she strode away.

***

Paul and Sandra were licensed opticians at Owl Optics. They managed a store at The Warehouse, a new commercial center on the site of a former box factory which now hosted startups and a World Food Court. Paul and Sandra had built an airy four-bedroom house in Turnball Heights. Their son, Milo, was the best in his group of gifted students. He read Spanish comic books and had already trounced his parents at chess. He still had the table manners of a ten-year-old though, stuffing his mouth with bread until his cheeks bulged and licking Monaco's arrabbiata sauce off his fingers. Later that evening, he surprised Paul by confiding that he was unhappy because another boy told him that he threw like a girl.

Paul consoled, "That's a stupid thing to say. Ignore him."

"Could you teach me to throw better?"

This was the first time that Milo had expressed such an interest. The garage was full of athletic gear that had gone unused. On vacations, Milo preferred to read in the Jacuzzi.

"Sure," Paul replied.

They went to the backyard and Paul tried to help him with his motion. Milo was a bit uncoordinated, but that could be addressed. Paul hadn't thrown hard since his freshman year in college, before a rotator cuff surgery had ended his pitching dreams. Now he tossed a gentle, slow overhand, encouraging Milo to learn sound mechanics. There was pleasure in these gestures, as well as an intimation of a larger game, with its difficult and unchanging rules. His phone vibrated in his pocket but he ignored it. Milo wasn't too good at catching the ball, either—it deflected off his glove then bounced off his chin—but he didn't complain or make excuses and, another time, he trapped the ball against his chest. "Good one!" Paul encouraged.

Back in the house, checking his phone, he saw that it was Bobby Carson. He put the phone back in his pocket. Later that same evening, when Milo was in the bath and Sandra was doing yoga on the back patio, Bobby called again.

"So I got in touch with the professor who was on TV," he an-

nounced. "Professor Spivak. Know what he said? He sees a stylistic resemblance in this cave painting to examples from the Upper Paleolithic
era. 'That is my hypothesis,' he said. Fuck, Paul! We could be in *National
Geographic!*"

Paul balked. "This can't last. Surely they'll do radiocarbon dating. Right?"

"Yeah, he did mention that. But for now, we're the toast of the
town. Since they ran the story, the professor has been contacted by lots
of places, it's going on national media. 'Stylistic resemblance!' I must've
learned something from Fat Fergie after all."

Bobby's tone, the assumed complicity—it was like a door had
opened onto a lost world. As if they were still kids, playing pranks and
laughing till their sides hurt. Fat Fergie had been their high school art
teacher, an obese man who wore colorful ties and tried to instill culture
with slideshows. Bobby had gotten kicked out of Mr. Ferguson's class for
ad-libbing voices for famous paintings. "Pull my finger," God demanded
from his throne on the Sistine Chapel's ceiling.

Paul tried to bring Bobby back down to Earth. "You don't seem
to understand. I have no desire to reminisce about Fat Fergie. I don't
care about the cave. All that is ancient history."

"I hear you, doctor! I'm talking about what next. Remember
those guys in England with crop circles? If we're smart, we could play it
like that, only bigger. The question is, when is the time to come forward
and take credit? How do we capitalize?"

Paul was taken aback. Capitalize? Hang on. Why should his
name be linked to this painting? There was his business at Owl Optics to
consider, his image in town. The past was full of dumb and regrettable
things that a normal person didn't want to revisit. He had no wish to be
associated with something so puerile. "Count me out." He switched off
his phone.

Mostly, though, he was thinking about Frances.

***

Bold—there was no choice but to be bold. Since Frances attended a different school, there weren't any built-in social opportunities or
courtship situations. They would never cross paths. So he had to seek her
out and assert his presence.

He went to one of her games, and then another, watching con-
tests between unfamiliar teams—a spy in a strange land—watching *her.*
And with astonishing ease, he learned all about Frances. The way she
carried herself in public, interacted with teammates, expressed joy or
frustration. He spent a lot of time studying her short, curvy body, the
lines of the uniform, her compact power. He even met her family...be-
cause the grandstand was full of Taluccis. Brothers and sisters, her curly-

haired mom and bald dad, a big-mouthed uncle (and another bald man) who bellowed, "Go-oo-oo, Franny!" There were so many Taluccis that Paul wondered about the transportation arrangements, if they had their own bus.

This was her world. So very different from Paul's. He had no siblings, and his parents, though supportive, were too busy to attend his games. His father's dental practice was booming and his mother played competitive bridge at high levels, attending her own tournaments. Maybe that fact had brought him closer to Bobby, whose parents had other priorities than baseball, too. The Carsons ran a heating and air-conditioning business. Bobby's father was always out in the van for an installation or a repair, while his mother managed the office and Bobby was expected to help with his little sister, Judy, who was a child with Down syndrome. Sometimes you'd see Bobby and Judy in front of the office downtown, on a bench near a traffic light, watching the world roar by, Judy licking an ice cream.

One Saturday, after seeing Frances strike out the last batter and win her game, Paul hurried down to the front row by the first-base line, where she would see him as she left the field.

"Good job!" he called.

She appeared surprised, but she walked straight to him.

"What are you doing here?"

"I came to see you."

"That right?" She smiled, and he felt a lightness such as he'd never known. As if he'd entered a new territory where shyness and limitations no longer existed. He could be frank and honest, because the only currency was hope.

"I need to talk to you, Frances. I need to see you."

"Like, *now?*"

She was still in uniform, dusty from the game, and in seconds they were surrounded by her family and friends who came to congratulate her. Suddenly he realized that she didn't even know his name. "I'm Paul."

***

"Who was that on the phone?" Sandra asked, rolling up her yoga mat. She wore iridescent purple leggings.

"I was talking to Bobby Carson."

"Really? I thought you didn't like that guy. Is he trying to sell you something?"

"Yeah. That's it."

It wasn't exactly a lie. Bobby had become a real estate agent, his face was on signs all over town. That's how Sandra knew about Paul's antipathy toward Bobby. Once, stopped at a red light, he noticed a sign and exclaimed, "Jesus, will that asshole ever go away?"

Sandra said, "But we don't want to buy anything."

"That's what I told him."

Sandra had gone to school in a St. Paul suburb, therefore knew nothing about what had happened. They'd met in an optometry course and settled here after they got married. Over the years, he'd never lied to Sandra. But he'd never mentioned Frances Talucci, either.

***

The first Saturday, the young couple went to see a movie; the following weekend, they watched the finals of a girls' softball tournament. Paul much preferred their second date because, unlike in the theater, where chase scenes and exploding fireballs occupied their attention, they could actually talk in the grandstands. Frances wore sandals, her toenails painted crimson—he often glanced at her small brown hands and feet, trying not to stare at her body—and she told him her opinions about umpires and last week's movie and why she was going to college to be a teacher and a coach. Paul told her of his plans to be a doctor. Frances seemed at ease with him, though Paul noticed that she was also chatty with spectators in nearby seats and with the guy who sold peanuts. Maybe it had something to do with being from a big family. People didn't spook her.

When they left the game, she took his hand on their way to the parking lot. They kissed when they said goodnight, which was both encouraging and bittersweet because the next day he was leaving town for two weeks to join his parents on vacation. When he came back, summer would be over, they would return to their different schools and seeing each other would become difficult. Paul had begged his parents to let him stay behind, but they would hear nothing of it.

For two weeks, Paul punished his parents in their cabin by a lake in northern Wisconsin by making a point of not enjoying himself. His father, Mitch, considered these retreats as a sacred, manly ritual, fishing and hiking in a favorite pair of old lace-up boots, far away from his dental practice, from TV and telephones; Paul's mother, Connie, sunned on the dock drinking rosé, her nose in a book. Paul spent his time moping indoors where he composed moony letters to Frances. One day, Paul and his father argued about starting a fire. Mitch prided himself on using only one match. If you arranged the chips and kindling correctly, one match was all it took. Mitch had explained his method and demonstrated its success. "See—just one." He smiled, pleased with his skill. This time Paul was preparing the chimney and he noticed that Mitch was observing closely, and he became aware that his father's opinion of him was at stake. Would he manage with only one match? Paul slowed down, giving his father an opportunity to look away or go do something else. But no, Mitch continued to watch him. A sudden intuition flowed through Paul, telling him that somewhere in Mitch's heart was a place—a place that maybe he didn't even realize existed—that would be *glad* if Paul failed. That way, he would remain secure in his superiority.

"Frances was still pretty, but her cheeks were puffed out. As if she were wearing a mask of herself that didn't fit quite right. Her eyes were smaller. She was fat, too. He didn't want to think these thoughts, but he did."

With a grunt, Paul seized a can of lighter fluid and carelessly doused the wood, struck several matches with a lazy swipe and tossed them on the pile. An audible clap—*whoosh!*—a huge gust of flame. Paul jumped back from the chimney. "The hell is the matter with you?" his father cried, stomping his boot.

Upon returning from vacation, he telephoned Frances but she was no longer available. "The truth is," she said, "I've started seeing someone else, and it wouldn't be appropriate. I'm sorry."

Paul was gutted. He blamed his parents. This wouldn't have happened if he'd stayed in town! And he was even less prepared for what came next. He assumed his rival was someone from Frances' circle, someone he didn't know. But a few months later, he gripped Bobby in a headlock and demanded to know if the rumors were true.

"I didn't mean to!" Bobby squirmed like a puppy. "We'd go to the cave and hang out. Her parents are strict as hell, there's no question of an abortion. That's what they say. My mom and dad are totally pissed and they say I have to step up to the plate."

To Paul's astonishment, Bobby expected his pity.

"There's no way out, man!" he added. "Sometimes I want to kill myself."

***

"He's a dirtbag," Paul told Sandra. "That's why I don't like him. See, I knew a fellow in high school, a nice guy. He had a girlfriend and Bobby wormed his way in and next thing you know, he gets her pregnant. Big-time stupid. Maybe it sounds like a cliché, but it's more than that. There were major consequences. This girl was a sweet kid, plenty of potential, the world was her oyster. And what happens is, she doesn't even finish high school, she wrecks her life to marry a jerk like Bobby and they have three kids, *bang-bang-bang*, before they turn around and get divorced and she has a bunch of other problems. A lot of grief. But Bobby's face is still smiling all over town. He's remarried with a new wife half his age. Okay, maybe ten years younger, I shouldn't exaggerate. But that's what I hear. The guy is always seeking attention and it gets under my skin."

Sandra waited a few seconds. "It was your girlfriend, wasn't it?"

Paul sighed, feeling lame. Was he that obvious? "Right. It was a million years ago and all very small-time. We barely dated. I feel silly even talking about it."

"That was the woman we saw in Crap Palace, wasn't it?"

Now he was startled. How did Sandra pick up on *that*? It was almost clairvoyant, creepy.

Of course, the store wasn't really called Crap Palace. That's just how they referred to it, a vast and ugly retail outlet on the edge of town. Paul and Sandra generally avoided the place and would never consider it for food shopping but occasionally stopped by to stock up on cleaning products and other household items. They got in and out as fast as they could. One Saturday, Paul was barreling along with a trolley stacked as high as his head with paper towels. Sandra was off somewhere filling her own trolley with tiki torches and mosquito repellent candles. Milo had parked himself on a bench in front of the customer service counter where he listened to a podcast on the Galapagos Islands (he had a thing about turtles). A slow-moving trolley ahead of Paul forced him to slow down. A woman dawdled in front of a pyramid of canned chili. It was Frances.

"Paul?"

"Well, hello."

His mind raced as they faced each other in the grainy blue fluorescent light. Frances was still pretty, but her cheeks were puffed out. As if she were wearing a mask of herself that didn't fit quite right. Her eyes were smaller. She was fat, too. He didn't want to think these thoughts, but he did.

"You must've made quite a mess," she remarked.

For a moment Paul was bewildered, and then he remembered his mountain of paper towels.

"A huge one!" he agreed.

She flashed a smile and he knew, *oh he knew*, how glad he was to see her. Years of stored-up feelings washed over him. He didn't know where they came from, it was strange; he could only suppose that the feelings had always been there. They chatted and, without mentioning Bobby Carson, she told him about her kids. The eldest, Robby, had graduated from high school three years ago and now worked a night shift at this very store. Paul could've said, *I heard a couple of years ago he was mixed up in a drug bust. Glad to know he's not in jail.* Her middle child, Kaylee, she told him, was in the Navy, presently stationed in Yokosuka, Japan. Paul could've replied, *When I was snooping on the Internet for information about you I found hardly anything except your DUI arrests but there were a lot of selfies of Kaylee who unfortunately doesn't resemble you.* Her youngest child, Garth, she said, was a high school senior. "Talk about a handful, let me tell you!"

Paul shivered. The air-conditioning at Crap Palace was always cranked to full blast. The place was like a slaughterhouse.

"Somebody's waving at you," Frances said.

He turned and saw Sandra at the end of the aisle, standing out from the rest of the clientele in her jodhpurs and silk scarf. Her trolley was full. She gave a quick thumbs up and pushed on toward the checkout counter.

"That your wife?" Frances asked.

"Yes."

"She's elegant."

"Yes, she is. Well...it was great talking to you."

That was months ago. Sandra hadn't said a word that day. But she'd remembered, and now she'd instantly made the connection to Bobby Carson. So why not confide the rest?

"Even if it was an immature teenage thing, I still wonder what

37.

she saw in him. It surprises me to this day. Bobby was a conniver. A weasel. I'm being objective here. What did he have to offer?"

Sandra laughed.

"Sometimes it's less what a guy has to offer than what he's ready to forget. For instance, scruples."

"He pretended he was my friend."

She shrugged. "Well, to be fair, he didn't act alone. You might think you're being gallant to stand up for your old sweetheart, but she made her choices, too."

Paul listened, he couldn't contradict her, exactly, but there was something incomplete or even patronizing in her description. No, it wasn't that simple. It was more complicated in the cave.

***

"Hey, doctor. How's it going?"

Paul raised his gaze from his computer screen. Bobby looked around the shop, all gleaming chrome and reflecting glass. There were no other customers, and he sat down across from Paul.

"We need to talk. You don't answer my messages."

"Go away, Bobby. I'm working."

"It's still about Franny, isn't it? For fuck's sake. I'd thought you'd moved on. How many years has it been? Just say what you want to say and get it off your chest."

Despite his irritation, Paul was also intrigued, impressed even, at Bobby's approach. Once again he'd called him *doctor*. How did he know about this sore spot? Was it instinct? He could smell a vulnerability and go straight to it?

Paul was no doctor. His father Mitch chuckled at Paul and Sandra's white lab coats, which were part of the value-added strategy of Owl Optics. It made the franchise appear serious, while charging more than competitors for the same eyeglass frames made in China.

"Cute bird," Mitch mocked, referring to the stitched logo of a bespectacled owl on their lab coat pockets.

Paul knew his dad was thinking (and thereby reminding Paul, whether he wanted to think about it or not) of Paul's struggles in college, including a D+ in organic chemistry. (Mitch had gotten an A in organic chemistry—he was actually quite fond of organic chemistry.) Yes, it was all true, Paul wouldn't deny it...though dropping out of pre-med was many years ago and he felt acutely that this truth fell short of doing justice to his life. When could his father let it go? Or why should a bullshitter like Bobby Carson address him as *doctor*? Paul's feet shuffled convulsively under his desk. *Stop telling me who I am!*

Sandra entered the shop, returning from her lunch break. Her expression told him that she could see his anger. "Come with me," he told Bobby. It was his turn for lunch. On their way out, Paul made introductions. "This is Bobby Carson. We've got a few things to discuss." Sandra shook Bobby's hand, and Paul watched them size each other up. Bobby's look of approval of Sandra's appearance was irksome. He felt a mad impulse to shove Bobby aside. "Let's go."

The World Food Court at The Warehouse commercial center was a short stroll from Owl Optics. Paul ordered spicy Indonesian noodles and Bobby decided on fish tacos. By the time they sat down with their meals under the atrium, Paul had regained his composure.

"Let's make one thing clear. I have nothing to get off my chest about Frances Talucci. That's all in the past and done."

"Easy for you to say." Bobby bit into his taco. "I got reamed on the child support by a lady judge." He swallowed. "If *I'd* done half the drunken shit that Franny pulled before she went on the wagon, I wouldn't even have partial custody. It was pure sexism, dude, and I will call it by its name."

Paul raised a palm. "I don't want to hear this."

"Fine—it's not what I came to talk about anyway. I want to show you these."

Bobby pulled out his phone and began to swipe through photos. "I've been doing some research. Look at that." He leaned forward and swiped. "And look at that. You seeing what I'm seeing?"

It was cave art. Paul had viewed similar images before, if not exactly the same ones. He twisted noodles on a fork, then raised them to his mouth. "What do you want me to say?"

"These are from Spain, they say around thirty thousand years old. If you put aside the ones with animals, which I haven't bothered to download here, and focus on the paintings with the people, it's freaky as hell. Look at the people. This blows my mind."

"What?"

Overhead, rain began to patter on the glass of the atrium.

"The resemblance, man! There—look at the arm. And there— the stick. *The bat.* They're playing, Paul."

It took a moment for these words to sink in.

"Baseball? That's what you're saying, Bobby? Ancient humans, running around in moss underwear, played baseball?"

"Go ahead and laugh. I didn't say it was baseball like ours. There are variations, you know. Jai alai comes from Basque country. These paintings are from that region, if you look at a map. This makes it more meaningful. Part of something bigger."

Paul ripped open a packet of pepper sauce. "That'll take some explaining. What are you driving at?"

"First, you're a condescending prick. Just so you know. Second, I'm saying there's more to what we did than meets the eye. There we were, two kids fooling around, and without knowing it, we tapped into

"We're not friends, I don't like him, but the thing is—what I'm trying to say—since he got in touch with me, it brought back so many emotions. I suppose I don't have many friends. I'm awfully busy."

something deeper. Way deeper. We captured an essence, bro. Here we are..." He took another bite of his fish taco and then used it to make a sweeping motion which took in the World Food Court. Rain kept drumming on the atrium's ceiling, competing with the piped jazz music playing in the background. Bobby continued, "...but we're connected, as sure as we sit here, with the dudes who did *that*." He nodded to the image on his phone. "It's the same shit. It's like they're speaking through us. Makes you think."

"Makes *me* think you spend too much time on the internet."

Paul expected another retort. But Bobby assumed a thoughtful air, even pious. "The big picture scares you, doesn't it? But I'm seeing this differently now. When we go public, we need to hit the right note and underline the connections. The cave is for real. It's *ours*, man. It's who we are. It's more than a joke, Paul."

Noodle sauce had dripped onto Paul's lab coat, and now he

rubbed at it with a paper napkin. "How many times do I have to tell you? Say whatever you want, but leave me out."

"So—I take all the credit. It's only me?"

"It's only you."

***

The rain abated in the afternoon but hit hard again that night, persisting into the morning. The Fourth Street Bridge was closed for public safety. This made for a longer, circuitous route to take Milo to his guitar lesson. And still, the rain didn't stop; there was flooding in the east part of town and in adjoining counties. For a week, logistics were a headache. The Warehouse was eerily quiet. The few shoppers inside wandered like lost souls haunting the shining storefronts.

Paul didn't hear from Bobby during this time. He spent hours filling out the annual self-assessment report for Owl Optics, about which goals had been met, and which areas needed improvement. He strained to imagine new goals that didn't echo last year's. Sometimes his mind drifted to his conversation with Bobby, and he wondered: *why does he seek my support or require my consent? What's in it for him? Won't the cave be the same without me?*

***

On Sunday morning, Paul and Sandra met his parents for breakfast. This was a monthly ritual at a downtown diner.

"I bet this handsome young man wants blueberry pancakes!"

Milo smiled at his grandmother, Connie. "That's right."

"And then he'll tell us about his girlfriends," Grandpa Mitch added huskily. "I betcha he's got lots of girlfriends!"

Milo looked down at the table, momentarily shy.

A woman named Heather served them. She was young and pretty and parried teasing from Paul's father with zingers of her own, feigning flirtation. Mitch always insisted on picking up the check and he informed servers in advance that he *might* leave a generous tip. The food arrived: eggs and low-carb fruit cups for the women, omelets and hash browns for the men. Meanwhile, Milo slathered his pancakes with syrup.

"You're not man enough to finish all that," his grandfather said. "Those pancakes are going to kick your ass."

Milo giggled.

They conversed briefly about the heavy rains until Milo

interrupted the adults to announce that he would recite the elements of the periodic table. Between bites, he rattled it off flawlessly, scarcely taking time to breathe. His grandparents looked on, concerned but ultimately approving.

Then they spoke of summer plans. Paul's father wanted to take the boy up to the cabin in Wisconsin. Milo had never been away from his parents for longer than a weekend.

"He'll love it! This boy's no noodle. Why, he'll catch his own walleye for breakfast every morning. You'd like that, wouldn't you, Milo?"

Milo nodded slowly. Connie stood up, clutching her purse, and excused herself. She didn't say where she was going, but Paul knew she was stepping outside for a smoke. Sandra excused herself, too. She would go keep Connie company. Paul's father carried on talking as if Milo wasn't supposed to notice his grandmother's cigarettes, but Milo noticed everything.

"You haven't been up to the lake for a while."

"That's true," Paul acknowledged.

"You should make time."

Paul emptied his coffee cup and put it down on the table. "We'll see."

"Milo," the old man said, "you gotta finish those pancakes. Show 'em who's boss!"

At that moment, Heather arrived with the check. Paul grabbed it before his father could take it. He stood up. "Come on, Milo. We're out of here."

"Hey, that belongs to me!" exclaimed Mitch.

"Nope." Paul counted out the tip.

"The hell is wrong with you?"

***

Bobby called the next day.

"Bad news, man."

"What do you mean?"

"It got flooded. The river left the banks and wiped out everything up to the picnic area. So the cave was under water for two days. There weren't resources to protect it. At least, that's what Professor Spivak says. The waters have receded and the painting is gone. He's pretty bummed. All he has is a photographic record so his research will have to limit itself to style. He's gonna publish the pictures."

"Didn't you tell him the truth?"

"Not yet."

There was a pause, and Paul pursued, "Are you going to?"

"It's like a legacy, right? Our style, I mean. And I want to protect it, include it in the record."

"But it's bullshit.

"It's part of us, man."

Paul said nothing.

"Besides," Bobby added, "the professor wants to get an article out of this real bad. He says it's for the sake of knowledge. Why disappoint him?"

Paul hung up.

***

JoJo's was a sandwich shop on the far south side of town. Paul arrived early and ordered an iced tea, trying to compose his thoughts. When Frances appeared, she wore a green shawl and her hair, still long and curly but streaked with gray, fell over her shoulders.

"Well, this was unexpected." She slipped into a chair. "I've got another appointment in half an hour so I don't have much time. What can I do for you?"

The phrase sounded forced. Another appointment. As he watched her unwrap her shawl, he doubted these words. Why was she so wary? It was true, though, that Sandra didn't know about this meeting with Frances. He might mention it later. That's what Paul told himself.

"Can I get you an iced tea? Maybe a sandwich?"

Frances shook her head. "I'm good."

A truck rumbled by, vibrating the windows. She looked at him, waiting.

"I wanted to check in with you," he said. "See how things are going." He tried to sound casual, as if this was something they did periodically.

"I'm fine, Paul. And you? How's your wife? You have a son, right?"

"Everybody's good." He placed his palms on the table. "My boy's doing great but he's getting to the age where he likes to push back."

A week ago, after they'd returned from the diner and Paul announced in unequivocal terms that Milo would *not* be joining his grandparents at the cabin, he responded by making a scene. Suddenly he wanted to go to the lake. "I don't get to do anything!" he cried.

"Uh..." Paul groped for an argument. "I need to teach you to swim first."

Milo stalked off to his room and slammed the door. He'd shut himself away every night that week. Sandra was surprised at Paul's decision. "Maybe we should let him go. He doesn't have many friends. He could use some growing up." Paul conceded that Milo spent too much time alone with his tablet. Now, as he picked up his glass of iced tea, it occurred to him that his son had started masturbating. He put down his glass and looked out the window.

"Funny you suggested this place," Frances said. "I meet here sometimes with Judy."

"Judy?"

"Yeah, you remember Judy. Bobby's sister? We keep in touch."

"Oh, right. How is she?"

"She works part-time at Morrisey's, not far from here. Judy's doing okay. She——" Frances cut herself off. "You didn't really know her, did you?"

Paul shook his head, trying to picture Judy as an adult. "Not really."

"I've always liked Judy." Now Frances became very still. "Paul, what can I do for you?"

"It's about the cave. What's happened to it. Has Bobby told you?"

She looked at him blankly.

"What cave?"

"You know—by the river."

Her expression turned into a scowl.

"Why would you bring that up? Why would I be talking to Bobby?"

"Well, you mentioned Judy——"

"That's different. She's like a sister to me, but Bobby's not worth my time."

Paul wished he could take back his words, the unwelcome images he'd conjured up, of the cave and old sleeping bags, the design scratched on stone. Did she know that he'd had a hand in the writing on the wall? Paul tried to erase the images.

"Oh, the place got flooded and it was on the news, that's all. Bobby talked to me about it. We're not friends, I don't like him, but the thing is—what I'm trying to say—since he got in touch with me, it brought back so many emotions. I suppose I don't have many friends. I'm awfully busy." Paul felt out of breath, as if he'd been running. "My family is great, I'm lucky there, though it's harder with my parents...my dad is a dick. Anyway, the point is—I'm reaching out. I guess I'm asking you to be my friend. You see?"

"You're acting weird, Paul. Why me?"

"Of course you! Frances, you know I like you. Honestly I'd like to fix this crazy world. We're not kids anymore, right?"

"Right. But why ask me? What do you want from me? Ask your wife." She looked at him intently, as if searching for the right spot. "Actually, it's not her problem. Ask Bobby. Your dad. You fuckers got some stuff to sort out. Don't come to us. Just do it."

Frances stood up and threw her shawl over her shoulders.

"Please. Can't you wait?"

"You want to fix the world, Paul? Go home."

Springtime Falls

Mike Lee

Katerina tasted metal in her mouth. Through the curtain half-pulled across the window, the clouds shielding the rising sun lent a dull grayness to the early morning. Katerina pulled the black sheet away and padded across the parquet floor into the bathroom. She remained on the toilet for fifteen minutes, looking at the shoe ads in a fashion magazine and cursing her age.

Katerina liked her chocolate-brown West Elm furniture, the bookshelves neatly arranged, the coffee table square and modern, the lamps cheaper than they looked, the framed prints on the wall: Magritte, Rothko, classic Frank Kozik posters from Austin in the early nineties, back when that city was fun, before California, Mexico, and New York moved in and fought for the couch. *Yes, New York*, she thought. *So I was going to be a writer.*

Manhattan. Katerina moved there in 1992 (she was twenty-seven), after graduate school and a job in publishing. Went straight to associate editor, promoted to senior editor in six months. Family money was still left over, and the pay was good, so she could afford the apartment at the edge of the East Village. It was on the L train, an easy commute from her stop on First Avenue and Fourteenth Street, zipping over to Union Square, then transferring to the Lexington 4/5 to get to Midtown before walking a single block and taking an elevator ride to the thirty-seventh floor.

Katerina dressed like the six digits she made. She liked her high-heeled Louboutins—even though they were hard to find without platforms (which made her feel like a stripper)—and the somewhat butch power suits featuring pencil skirts or pants designed and tailored on the Rodeo Drive of wealthy hipsters: Ninth Street in the East Village. Katerina was five-foot-one and a little on the zaftig side, with streaks of gray fighting her auburn hair for space. Therefore, she required a look that exuded her authority, albeit not much more than stage managing three different lifestyle magazines for a company on the edge of collapse between the twin plagues of endless recession and the internet. Katerina built her design skills and had her resume ready in 2008, but she knew better. Forty-seven had become the new sixty in this postmodern economy, so she obsessively checked the stock portfolio from her parents' trust fund and the investments made with the money left by her grandparents. She had a 401K that got dented, *hard*, from the crash, but it remained enough to pay whatever capital gains taxes she would have to...and there was always Texas.

Texas. Home, though Austin and the surrounding Hill Country, had changed dramatically. The house, to her, represented Mom and Dad in a suburb overlooking Lake Travis, going to football games with her best friend and punk rock shows at Raul's and Club Foot. All that had gone away now—consigned to nostalgic sentimentality on Facebook. Katerina was wise to reread her diaries. It was one matter that the bands she saw left more of an impression than the people in her life, quite another that the daydreams expressed in cursive on college-ruled lines were invariably better than her daily reality...then *and* now.

When she returned to Austin—and Katerina was somewhat resigned that she would—it would be to a skyline like Houston without Philip Johnson, expensive restaurants rivaling Manhattan's price and sprawl. The little suburban community she knew at thirteen had turned into a sea of built-up mansions over every hill. Even the house she grew up in had been torn down in the mid-2000s for a horror of French whatever, complete with driveway fountain. It made her sick to see it, considering her father had designed the original neighborhood when the first spades struck. On the other hand, there was still excellent barbeque to be had, which she missed, and the music scene was worthwhile, meaning she wouldn't mind being the middle-aged lady rubbing shoulders with her peers who had decided to stay. Most importantly, she could afford to live there, and being lonely in the sun in Texas was far better than dying alone in New York. She needed to leave, but vowed to hang on until she could no longer.

Katerina unrolled her mat and began her pilates, stretching in her bra and panties. After another hour lifting weights, she retired to the shower, scrubbed and cleaned, then put on red shorts and a white ribbed tank top, relics from when she used to work out at the gym. She stopped going last year when she realized she could do everything at home, and the girls around her were getting younger while the older ones were flailing against the brick wall of the calendar. Katerina preferred to wrap her insecurities in a blanket. She liked her legs just the way they were and, while a little flabby in the middle and saggy ever so slightly in the rack, Katerina still enjoyed the attractiveness of her body. It was her face that she had issues with. It seemed everything wrong went there. Her forehead furrowed like the rivers of Mars and her crow's feet, sprung from decades of eye strain, were more and more apparent. She accepted this as part of her transition into middle age; fighting reality would only add to the stress. She had a coworker, Evelyn, who had already undergone surgery. Evelyn looked so stretched out that she reminded Katerina of her cat. She wasn't going to embarrass herself, that much Katerina resolved by applying makeup every morning and cold cream every evening. She also took pride in her looks, telling herself these were marks of experience. Just not today. She did not want to look at herself on her self-imposed mental health holiday. But, in the end, of course she did.

Katerina sat behind her vanity table and brushed her hair, gazing at her own face as she did so. Her glasses were off, so the softness from her aging vision buffeted her sensitive nature as she untangled wet, wavy locks before rising and moving into the living room. Katerina toasted a bagel in the kitchen and made coffee. She picked up the remote and clicked on the stereo, listening to R.E.M.'s *Murmur* (college days music) without much sentiment. More sentimental to Katerina were Simple Minds and The Damned. R.E.M. was nothing but orchestrated elevator music. Listening to these songs now as MP3s or playing old videos on YouTube brought out mixed emotions. She still snickered, however, over the goofy lyrics of "Pilgrimage." Twenty years after first hearing the song, she continued to think the opening included the directive, "Take out the washing." She hummed to the words, "Your hate, two-headed cow," then munched on her bagel.

She spent the morning doing laundry downstairs and taking dry cleaning over, stopping off at Starbucks for her Venti coffee, and then an hour watching a game of squash, sitting anonymously in the shade under blue skies. Her phone was on mute, steadfastly refusing to take calls from her neurotic assistant, Deidre. Katerina felt like smoking a cigarette. She had smoked a pack a day from high school until graduate school part two, as it were, and gave it up when she moved to New York. Too expensive these days. The urge returned on occasion, but this was the first time in years she'd felt a nicotine craving come on, albeit a mild one. Katerina was surprised; she did not know where that came from, remembering it had also occurred during her anxiety attacks before she went into therapy, was prescribed medicine and learned yoga.

That was fifteen years ago, which Katerina termed the Middle Ages, while her time in Texas was the Classical Age. Katerina timed her life in epochs, framing her regrets as chapters in history.

She wasn't any closer to being a writer than she had been when

"Katerina had her experience with the fancy and pretentious, but at heart, she was a good Texas gal with simple needs when taking her 'solo act' out into the open. She was, in a word, boring, but Katerina did not mind. Security was more important than excitement. Sometimes, however, she locked herself in the bathroom and cried."

she decided to make a go of it in the big city. Shortly after breaking up with Manny, she had been sitting behind the railing at Captain Quackenbush on the Drag, drinking a double iced cappuccino, and a bum had walked by and handed her a book, advising, "This is something I think you ought to read."

It was *Story of the Eye* by Georges Bataille, and it was then that Katerina decided to get the fuck out of Austin, away from Texas, and travel beyond the edge of the known world. Yes, being handed a book—especially *that one*—was enough to say, *That's it.*

Katerina consoled herself that she had left not because her two great loves failed or she felt alienated from her circle of friends—no, it was a *dragworm*, of all people, handing her a novel as she sipped her double iced cap. No man or woman would drive her from home into northern island exile.

So she named her cat Manny and her MacBook Sherry. Sherry being what passed for her high school sweetheart: dysfunctional at heart, dominating, manipulative, needy and clueless. Sherry was edited from Katerina's sexual experience biography whenever it still mattered. Struck from the book—what the hell, it was a long, long time ago. The Middle Ages, not relevant to her Modern Day forty-whatever... except when she decided to express her dom side, slipping into latex, and heading off to the spanking club. Katerina once gave a brilliant lecture about BDSM to a bachelorette party.

Katerina was interested in one of the partygoers, a gawky blond, but couldn't bring herself to ask to kiss, to connect. Instead, Katerina talked her into the cage and cranked her to the ceiling, giggling along with the other women. But when she stared at the blonde clutching the cage bars nervously, Katerina saw herself at seventeen again and doing whatever Sherry told her to do. So she turned the crank in the opposite direction, bringing her back down to cracked concrete and watching her click away in cheap platforms. Katerina told herself the blonde *probably, possibly* would have been interested, but Katerina had already stepped away from the cliff. "Mistress Kat" went back into the closet, on a hanger behind the prom dress from 1982. She thought about that young woman, though. Blonde, asymmetrical cut with bangs, angular, thin and tall, tall, tall. She was the type who *so* did what she was told.

Manny would *never* do what Katerina *wanted* to tell him. In one of her old journals, she had listed everything she wished she had said to him when they were together. Remembering the first entry still hurt her mind, where regret and stupidity resided as neighbors. *If you like it, put a ring on it.* After waiting forever for him to do what she wanted without having to verbalize it, Katerina left...over the fence, into the fields, through the mountains, across the river, to the shore and beyond the sea. Back to Sherry, but only briefly, because returning to teenage vomit was always a mistake. Plus, Sherry went off her meds and it all turned into codependent, woo-woo-moonbat crazy bitch bondage, and Katerina finally figured out that Sherry just really hated women.

After abandoning Sherry, Katerina gleaned two critical lessons from her experience. Number one, if it was terrible the first time, leave it alone. And number two, she would not understand women until she figured herself out. Those were the days *lost, lost, lost, lost, lost—*

She froze. *Did I remember my meds? Shit.* Chest tightened, cramps rolling like cookie dough across her shoulder blades, left eye fluttering. She really hoped it was an anxiety attack. But unfortunately, she was not self-assured at her age and with her family history. *Breathe, Katerina, breathe.* Chest rising, remembering she still had a clean bill of health from the last exam. *Repeat to yourself: it ain't happening.*

Breathe. Breathe. Katerina closed her eyes, palms up, dropping her arms to her sides. *Wipe free the thoughts from thy mind, travel to the grayness of oblivion, which no one who hurts may enter. Try not to think. In other words, just shut up.*

Katerina rose from the bench and went inside her building. She unrolled her mat at home on the living room floor, played meditative music and worked through her old yoga positions. It calmed her, focusing her energies, centering as if by rote. After an hour or so of working herself, clutching her ankles, mind blank, Katerina rolled up the mat and took a bath. It was still morning, close to eleven, and she already felt she had had a long day. After soaking, she decided to "get pretty" before going off to wander. Katerina could still pull off white capris, leather gladiator sandals and a red silk blouse (late May was warmer than usual for a Manhattan spring). The anxiety attack pissed her off. She had to put up with the twinges for a while, even after she belatedly took her Ativan. She should *not* have flashed back to Sherry, but twenty years later, the nasty bitch continued to squat rent-free in her mind. *It sucks, but sometimes that's just how it is,* Katerina reminded herself while waiting for the bus on the corner of Avenue A.

She had forgotten her headphones. Alas, the bus was already coming down Fourteenth Street, so Katerina shrugged and pulled out her MetroCard. She made her way to the back, standing instead of sitting beside a corpulent woman breathing heavily, half her ass covering a third of the remaining available seat. Katerina pushed her sunglasses to the top of her head and leaned coolly against the pole by the rear door.

She reached into her bag, pulling out her book. Katerina had gotten back into Ernst Jünger, having read Roberto Bolaño's references to his work in *The Savage Detectives* and *2666,* and had to search online for a copy of her favorite novel of his, *On the Marble Cliffs,* finding the first Penguin printing for thirty bucks used. At Union Square, she stepped away to avoid the crowd emptying out, found a single seat on the left-hand side, plopped down and continued reading to Abingdon Square by Ninth Avenue. Katerina exited at the bus stop by the park, walked north to Fourteenth and entered Chelsea Market (what used to be the Nabisco factory).

Since it was a Tuesday, the shops weren't as crowded, so she didn't have to wait in line (or "on line") too long to pick up some Swiss cheese, her favorite stone ground wheat crackers, a Soho vanilla cream soda and ripe grapes. Katerina moved through the market, with its décor in rusted post-punk metal, to the rear entrance and the stairwell leading up to the High Line. Katerina especially liked the walk at night, but the cloudless blue sky and temperature in the eighties made coming up in the daytime sound appealing.

She went to a table in the shade and began eating her snack/lunch, sipping her soda through a straw, and checking out the tourists, attempting to guess their country or state of origin. Most coming to

> "She wasn't any closer to being a writer than she had been when she decided to make a go of it in the big city. Shortly after breaking up with Manny, she had been sitting behind the railing at Captain Quackenbush on the Drag... and a bum had walked by and handed her a book, advising, 'This is something I think you ought to read.' It was *Story of the Eye* by Georges Bataille."

New York these days were German, though she swore from the accents there was a tour group from Alabama.

It was relatively simple, her cheese and crackers. Katerina had her experience with the fancy and pretentious, but at heart, she was a good Texas gal with simple needs when taking her "solo act" out into the open. She was, in a word, boring, but Katerina did not mind. Security was more important than excitement. Sometimes, however, she locked herself in the bathroom and cried.

Yes, *cried*. No kids, no relationship, no published work beyond occasional short stories…she hadn't even bothered to do a public reading since the late nineties. She worked in obscurity, lived in isolation and had become faceless (though she still had a pretty face, despite the lines of the early Middle Ages). She munched wistfully on cheese and crackers at her metal table, thinking about the people she missed—starting with Manny. Was he the love of her life? She pondered that yet again. *Maybe I should just say fuck it and move to Singapore and teach English,* she thought.

Grow old as the crazy lady; maybe keep parakeets. Probably couldn't take the cat. "But I love my cat," she murmured. "So, Texas it is. Home, after a fashion."

"Manny. Maynard. Boy. Girl." Katerina stared ahead, stared inside herself through a telescope, standing in a snowy field. She breathed, shut her eyes, and added, tongue rolling over the words, "Us. Together. We. Then, no more. Alone." She placed her hands on her knees. Three and a half years of her life in an eleven-word mantra. Twenty years after they broke up, memories of Manny were painfully consigned to journaling and dozens of sessions with three consecutive therapists boxed inside little rooms throughout various locations in Lower Manhattan, so she stripped the story to single-word bursts of postmodern eloquence, as if that were more than just an avoidance ritual, keeping her from expressing what she felt. *Manny, Maynard, My One, That Boy, The Boyfriend* began as a novel in her mind and is now a shopping list on a notepad, torn and jammed, folded, in a pocket.

That's right, she still missed Manny, who had moved on—married with children—and was blocked by Katerina on Facebook because she did not want to see because it hurt to know. She was missing Sherry, too. Neither was meant to be, which left Katerina with her cheese and crackers on the High Line. Alone—yeah, that's it—alone. Katerina thought of a word she had learned from Manny the night they met—*kissless*. Perhaps she should use it in another short story that would be completed, sent out and rejected. Until then, it was a description of what she had become. Katerina smirked. Five years since she'd been with a guy and seven since she'd been with a woman.

She mused, *Consider me, as usual, bi-furious, or just plain fucking rejected—two years, four months and a week in therapy since it was the overriding theme. Yes, dear Katerina, always kissless until tomorrow, tomorrow never comes, and tomorrow is forever eternal until nothing more tomorrow.*

Katerina neatly folded the wax paper seal over the cheese and closed the cracker box, placing them, along with the grapes, in her bag. She rose from the table, her stomach slightly upset, slipped on her sunglasses and sauntered into the northern breeze. With Jersey on the left and Manhattan on the right, Katerina thought once more about the idea of returning Texas. *You can't, Kat,* her interior voice told her. *There is no home there anymore.*

As if possessed, she suddenly shouted, "In New York, my ghosts keep me company! Ghosts don't talk back! They do not hurt me! They never leave me, so I am never alone!" She looked around her, contentedly noted the judgmental stares and smiled.

Motivational Speaker

Max Talley

I am a commencement speaker; I try to motivate. Do you think this an easy task in our troubled times? No, I must use all my enthusiasm, energy and deep well of resources to rise above the encrusted muck we dwell in. Young adult graduates need to have hope to stagger forward into the unrelenting headwinds of our modern world. My discourse must launch over their heads like multicolored fireworks to dazzle them, to make them forget the student debts that will haunt them for the indeterminate future. I have to convince them that our rapidly heating planet of melting glaciers and rising sea levels is a bountiful place of unlimited opportunity for those with vision and tireless drive. Sometimes it exhausts me. I can't lie...rather, I must scrupulously avoid the truth.

I endeavor to speak at graduations every year, but nothing is ever certain. Sometimes I'm imprisoned by the very projects which make me worthy to be chosen. Arriving at Thanatos University, there is the usual confusion when the faculty meet me. For whatever reason, writers, poets and professors in academia often use photos taken years ago, if not decades earlier. Vanity perhaps, or more likely absent-minded negligence. The bearded, mountain man poet advertised to speak may now be a withered, white-haired codger leaning forward onto a cane. Life is cruel. Thankfully I'm not quite there yet. The photos I use as promotion vary in vintage, but someone always gives me a startled glance, trying to match my reality with the photograph. I am a changeable person who looks different from year to year. Once I show my ID and brandish one of my books, people generally shut up. Aging affects us all and humans rarely live up to their promotional images or social media photos.

An earnest female undergraduate named Breanne drives me from the train station to meet with the dean. College campuses are at their best in early June, the leafy trees sprouting on the manicured commons lawns and stately red brick buildings rising, a clock tower chiming in the distance. Connecticut, Massachusetts, New Hampshire? I am sometimes confused during graduation season. All lovely states of New England that are apparently dull as dishwater to actually live in. Best experienced as a day visitor.

"What made you switch from writing poetry to historical nonfiction?" Breanne asks me.

I stare out her Toyota's window, reminding myself exactly who I am and of my many accomplishments. "All writing is learning," I reply. "And all good writing is teaching." When I glance over at her, she's visibly confused, but chooses to keep quiet for the remainder of our drive.

I enter an administration building, its insides all dark wood and polished brass. Ushered into Dean Husk's office, I sit facing his desk, while a woman waits off to the side, studying me intently, as if to see through me.

Husk looks up from his paperwork. "Welcome." Taking in my height, he adds, "I expected you'd be taller." The woman glares at him, leading Husk to correct, "I meant...from old pictures of you standing next to Obama, and with civic leaders." He coughs. "We're not sizeist here."

"Good." I smile at both of them.

Husk flaps a single page. "As required by our board, we previewed your speech for today." He pauses, clears his throat. "Seems fine, but is this it?'"

"I start from a planned statement, one page, then I extemporize, like all the great thinkers and artists who inspired me."

"I see." He takes a deep breath. "Luna here is an administrator."

I swivel. "Oh, what do you do?"

Her face flinches. "I administrate."

"Of course."

"Times have changed," Husk continues, "since you began giving commencement speeches two decades ago, especially in recent years."

Luna nods, her face a stern mask.

"We strongly prefer you not touch on the Founding Fathers. They are, of course, problematic." He frowns as if chewing on a bitter memory. "We once had a speaker who referred to our graduating class as 'young ladies and gentlemen.'"

Luna shakes her head disapprovingly. "Please just address the graduating class as a singular body."

I scratch my hair, then cross my legs. "You know I'm a liberal from my writing, and a proponent of free speech, what with absurd book banning in Florida and other states. I'm allowed to mention the benefits of open minds and free speech, no?"

Husk half-smiles while Luna remains serious.

"My discourse must launch over their heads like multicolored fireworks to dazzle them, to make them forget the student debts that will haunt them for the indeterminate future. I have to convince them that our rapidly heating planet of melting glaciers and rising sea levels is a bountiful place of unlimited opportunity for those with vision and tireless drive. Sometimes it exhausts me."

"Of course you can." Husk pauses. "But at Thanatos University, we define free speech as anything our professors agree with."

I stay silent.

"That should give you some latitude," Luna adds. "We only share these concerns since part of your address will be...spontaneous."

"Best not to mention the former president either." Rusk scratches his lip. "Some alumni parents who are quite generous with annual donations to TU are, um, also his supporters." He flinches.

"Waste my time on the Manchurian Cantaloupe? No, never."

I stand, tired of academic rules and regulations. All these hoops to jump through for a modest payment. "I'm here to inspire the youth," I assure. "I have no interest in discussing religion, war or domestic politics. Just a positive message that is so needed nowadays. Lead me to the podium. I require only a glass of water." I unfold my one-page speech from my jacket pocket and flash it, to show it's the same one they preread. In a moment of levity, I elbow-bump Dean Husk as we both wear sports jackets with elbow patches.

Half an hour later, I lean on the lectern atop a low stage outdoors. Rows of seats fan out in front, with seniors—some in cap and gown, others casually dressed—and their parents in formal attire. Attentive, eager faces await my wisdom, as well as bored professors and hungover students desperate for the school year to be over. The weather is perfect: seventy-five degrees with a gentle breeze.

"Greetings," I announce into the microphone, pleased to hear it echo off the brick buildings in the quad. "Today I speak to a graduating class, both of..." I stop myself before saying "men" or "women." "I mean, to the amorphous sacks of protoplasm gathered." Youthful laughter sounds, and a stern professor takes off his glasses to squint at me. "You have been blessed to receive the best, or at least the most expensive education that money can buy." More titters and chuckles, while various parents lean forward, their expressions pinched.

"You have been given the skills over the past four years," I make random eye contact with a thick-necked jock, "or five or six years, to go out and make something of yourselves. To change a world that desperately needs changing. My generation tried. It succeeded in some areas and failed in others. You are aware of that, and now is your time to shine, to make the improvements in humanity we could not. For that, I thank you in advance and salute you."

Such a generic statement usually receives a rousing applause, and today is no different. I am soon done with my notes and start riffing on ideas, improvising like the jazz musicians I listened to inside. I so want to tell them they are leaving the last safe place, where their food and clothes and drugs and alcohol are all paid for. That they will enter a world where a high-salaried position may await, but they could easily end up living with their parents until middle age or work as an assistant manager at Target. Noticing Luna's laser-like stare from the front row, I restrain myself.

"Equity, diversity, inclusion." Then I say it again louder, fist pumped to the sky. Many stand to give me an ovation. Strange, on a college campus that means everything, yet at a job interview when a corporate VP announces it as company policy, it will mean absolutely nothing. Lip service.

"We must all help one another, the young and old," I insist to beaming faces. "And always choose freedom over tyranny. How can we contribute something positive to society?" At this point in speeches, I notice glazed eyes, heads lolling to the side, as various students scroll through their social media feeds. A perfect graduation Instagram photo will be essential.

"I have written collections," I continue. Audience members

nod. "The summer yawns before us, both eternal and gone in a flash. Should you find yourself walking the beaches of Cape Cod or Long Island, and a young woman passes by, don't be afraid to reach out and touch her bikinied breast..." Gasps and groans emanate from the crowd, faces turn as if to judge others' reactions. "With poetry," I finish. "For beneath the breast is the heart, and only the best poetry can penetrate there." A smattering of applause sounds. The irritation has subsided, though confusion still swirls about. Déjà vu. I've seen this before.

"You are now adults with new privileges, but also added responsibilities. Should you shop in a crowded supermarket or store and see a loud child misbehaving, their parents indifferent, take it upon yourself to spank the damn kid. Such as it was before, so shall it be again." I see people rise from their folding chairs; Luna confers with Dean Husk and other professors in a huddle. "Please, please, this is not harsh," I say. "For here in New England, are we not descendants of witch burners, of religious zealots who humiliated people in public stocks?" I start to hear loud boos.

"Remember, we are all graduates of the liberal arts. As liberals, we must never be ashamed of being black or brown, or white." Students and faculty chant to drown me out and the Colonial Studies professor storms off toward the parking lot.

I spot the van from my facility idling in the near distance. Attendants in scrubs smoke cigarettes, preparing to make their move. "Don't vote for bronzed tyrants wearing adult diapers who throw temper tantrums." A phalanx of administrators has formed to advance toward me on the stage. They realize I am an impersonator. I used to get through entire speeches before discovery. Must be slipping. My prosthetic nose itches like hell. "I am Batman..." Feedback sounds, then the public address system abruptly switches off.

It's so much harder now with facial recognition cameras and everyone carrying smartphones. I spend considerable time crafting disguises, trying to adopt the mannerisms of my subjects. They are temporarily imprisoned, completely unharmed, with food and drink until my charade ends. May I tell you, the buzz of public speaking is intoxicating.

The university will quash as much publicity as it can, since my speech can only serve as an embarrassment and might affect future endowments. I turn to run as they give chase, Dean Husk in the lead. They'll catch me, but a performance artist must not leave out any aspect of the ritual. Sure, I'll be locked up inside for a time. Though by next June, I envision commencement speeches in the Southwest or perhaps North Dakota, where northeastern regional news items rarely penetrate the public consciousness. Yes, I motivate people—in so many different ways.

POETRY

Tutankhamun

John Delaney

There's not a lot to say, strange as it seems.
I was a boy, expected to be king.
Yet I never got that far in my dreams.

They tell me my tomb was filled with treasure—
elaborate masks, furniture and toys,
some eighty pairs of golden sandals!

But I was mummified the same way:
a hook drew my brain out through my nostrils.
It was deemed useless in the Afterlife.

Other organs were removed and preserved in jars.
But not my heart, the seat of my soul.
It still had to pass the white feather test.

If your heart weighed less than the feather of truth,
you were judged a good man, welcomed to paradise.
I got an exemption, given my youth.

*Tutankhamun, popularly called King Tut, ruled Egypt from 1332 to 1323 BC, from the
age of nine to nineteen. During his reign, the traditional religion of Egypt was restored and
the capital moved to Thebes. The cause of his death is still debated.*

The Box Maker of Fares

John Delaney

These hardy boxes of dried palm tree fronds
are mainly used to carry mangos
from harvest to market, their craftsman says.
His feet keep a stave moving as he talks,
seeming to punch holes without looking.
He's sixty-one and has been making these
for fifty years. About four thousand a year,
as well as furniture and tourist trinkets.
So effortless and comfortable,
he works as if there's no such thing as work—
just satisfaction in doing something well.
It brings an income, has longevity:
everything that work can be if it has love,
and he labors with it as we listen.

Apparently, this man is well-known in Egypt, for his mango boxes are seen up and down the Nile.

Karnak

John Delaney

Temple upon temple upon temple,
gated fortresses of the spirit,
some yet to be discovered. A mental

walk among the crowds and ruins,
savoring the scent of ancient stone.
I looked up at the towering columns

and imagined one slightly off-balance,
slowly tipping, setting off a cascading
fall of dominoes; by a second glance,

though, they still stood solidly attentive
to their hieroglyphic narratives
in which, for centuries, they have lived,

both lifting and bearing the messages.
I was led to believe that something
as unwavering always blesses us,

like cupping brilliant sunlight in my hands.

*An overwhelming complex of temples, Karnak dates from the nineteenth to the third
centuries BC. Included are numerous statues, an obelisk and a hall of over one hundred and thirty columns. Excavation continues.*

The Camel Market at Daraw

John Delaney

He clutches the baby camel
as if he'll never let him go.
But of course he will. One day. Here.
The camel's a commodity.

The older ones bunch in small groups
with hobbled forelegs. Men come by
and whack them on their haunches,
trying to gauge their meat with sticks.

The heat's becoming uncomfortable,
but the camels would never know it.
Most of the men talk at tables
in the shaded open-air huts.

The boy leaning on the palm tree
is this owner's teenage son,
listening to learn what it takes
to be the best camel trader.

The best advice is to love them,
holding them tight for as long as you can—
the calf as well as the camel,
the boy who will carry the man.

Daraw is one of the two large camel markets in Egypt. Most of the camels come from Sudan and are sold for meat.

The Galabeya Tailor of Esna

John Delaney

Galabeya, sounds like it spells—
the standard dress of a working
Egyptian man, whether in the fields
or the shops. Long and loose-fitting.
The old tailor wears one himself.

Two blocks from the Temple of Knum,
god of the source of the Nile,
he works at his Singer machine,
shoeless and nimble-fingered,
sewing the seams of the garment.

Not fashion, not a uniform.
An everyday necessity
no one has to think what to wear.
Go in the shop and pick your cloth.
Get measured for a custom fit.

Wrap a turban round your head
to highlight the nobility,
so, when it's ready, you can walk out
among your peers dressed like a god
who has garbed responsibilities on Earth.

*In the hot summer, a white galabeya is common; winter colors include gray, tan, olive
and shades of blue.*

65.

Black or Red

Steve Denehan

There was no reason
for us
to feel out of place
but
we did

the casino was busy
three-quarters full
of people
who felt
right at home

I had expected the air
to be different
stretched tight
with pensions, homes, marriages
on the line

it was not
it was mundane
coin-toss futures
easy come
easy go

we had agreed to put $100 down
on black
or red, and then
walk away
regardless

$100
was something to us, and we
were nervous
grinning our way
to the roulette table

my wife looked at me

I told her to choose
black, or red
a binary decision
that took longer than it should have

she chose black, and
we won
or
more accurately
did not lose

Survivalists

Steve Denehan

I am a survivalist
in that
I am surviving, but
there are survivalists
of another kind
those who dig
deep down
to create
underground bunkers

this is appealing
to me

my bunker would be simple
filled with books and candles
enough non-perishable food
to last several decades
a CD player
a backup CD player, and
another CD player
just in case

there would be a fridge
a washing machine
an oven, and
of course
a generator
powered by aboveground
solar panels and wind turbines

there would be pencils, paper
paints and brushes
maybe a cactus
or two

I believe
that I could see out my days
in the bunker
happily, and easily, but

even then
I would consider myself
a survivalist
of a different kind

living in a bunker
not because the world has ended
but because it hasn't

Just Off Grafton Street, a Long Time Ago

Steve Denehan

The cobbles were slick
the rain was loud
we sat under an awning
just off Grafton Street

people hurried by
I watched them
you talked

most of the people
were office people
wore office clothes

some had umbrellas
most just turned
their collars up

rainwater quick-dripped
from the corner
of a parking metre
and the handlebars
of an old bicycle

it frothed
from a gushing gutter
to run across the path
the office people
stepped over it

I noticed the back of my hand
as if for the first time
it looked delicate
effeminate
a child's hand

you asked
if I was listening
I said that I was

Somewhere in the Universe

John Grey

You affect me still,
though it's been years.

Believe me...those winning charms
bewitch me now,
as you reach from the past,
      are cherished
      even on this latter day.

I blame your loose attire,
      the one sweet song
      we listened to
      conjoined,
that turned easy listening
into Apollo rocket—
      a priceless transformation,
      part me, part you:

even now, being in my orbit,
suits you.

Such things should happen.
That's why there's a moon. And stars.

I will always make room for
anything not of this Earth

Hunt

Megan Cartwright

Catch the scent, hackles rise.
Thinks I don't see.
Stay low. Stay secret.
Meat memory. Salivating.

Meat memory, salt-slick skin.
Snarling, froth and spittle.
I like to crunch the bones, suck the marrow.
Panting.

Replete.
Calcite deposits collect on canines.
Rattling breath; white pain of incisors.
Replete. Sink in sleep.

Alice in Training®

Bridget Kriner

No cloud was in the sky & no birds flying
overhead, there are no birds to fly
You first become aware & alert,
overcome denial. His contemptuous chortles
echo in the tones of a shark. His frumious footfalls
approach & you glimpse the vorpal metal in his hand
appearing smaller than its actual size.
The stuck voice in your throat quivers, timid & tremulous.
Manxome foe with eyes of flame lurks in wait
& appearing much further away than he actually is,
galumphing past the lockers, like the dog or the cat,
hunting for a rat. You think
I know who I was when I got up this morning,
but I think I must have been changed several times since.
You learn to break a window from the top corner
as opposed to the center, to expertly create movement,
distance and disturbance, you prop up
mimsy barricades while the slithy doorknob
equivocates *it is impassible; nothing is impossible.*
You talk of many things like why the sea is boiling hot &
whether pigs have wings when seconds count.
Information needs to be in clear, plain language.
You were curiouser it was in those moments,
so might just as well say that *I see what I eat*
is the same thing as *I eat what I see.*
Evacuation appears nearer than it actually is
You think, *I must be mad or I wouldn't have come here,*
which is true, or maybe just an altered perception
of time, as it seems almost brillig even though
you know it's much earlier in the day. You look up
in the midst of uffish thought when you hear
a barbarous walrus say, *I weep for you.*
I deeply sympathize, which is most likely
just zoopsia settling in, but still you wonder how
in our country, we could ever get through the rabbit
hole if *we only run very fast for a long time*
as we've been doing.

When I Watch True Crime Documentaries on Netflix

Bridget Kriner

Morbidly witnessing, I can't turn away,
draw shallow breaths to the tune
of tense piano, down-tempo electronica
with staccato strings & pulsating percussion.
My eyes mostly covered in palms,
cautious to see only the snippets
squeezing past the cracks in my fingers.
Clever detectives note every hair,
every errant fiber, blood-tinged footprints
in the snow, splatter distance & subtle hesitation
marks. All the pieces matter.
My craving for *why* is insatiable,
until I plunge an ordinary kitchen knife
in the heart of fascination, which just lies
there disemboweled, depravity unfurling
as blood pools under my shoes.

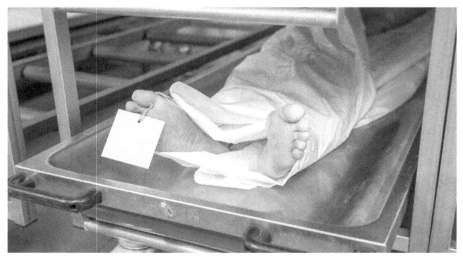

No Joke

Bridget Kriner

A man walks into a bar and asks the bartender for a glass of water. The bartender pulls out a gun and points it at the man. The man says, thank you and walks out. A man arrived to a gun fight with nothing other than a pencil and paper. He then proceeded to draw his weapon. How many guns does it take to change a lightbulb? Just one. Why did the gun cross the road? It musket to the other side. Knock. Knock. Who's there? Gun. Gun who? *Bang. Bang. Bang.* What do you call a baby gun? Son of a gun. A gun, a priest and a rabbi walk into a bar. The bartender says, *Shoot! I am not falling for this one again.* What do a bag of chips and a gun have in common? When you pull one out in class, everybody wants to be your friend. I don't like the word gun; whenever I say it, people always get triggered. I shot that guy with a paintball gun just to watch him dye. Why did the man bring a gun to the clock factory? To kill some time. What do you call an avocado that got shot? Glockamole. Due to the rising cost of ammunition, there will be no warning shots. What do you call a cat with a gun? A Mauser. What do you call babies with guns? Infantry. What do you call a sheep with a machine gun? Lambo. What gun does a military chef use? A salt rifle. I went to test my new gun at the range, but couldn't make it work; now I am troubleshooting. I think my wife has been putting super glue on my gun collection. She denies it, but I'm sticking to my guns. What do you call a fisherman fishing with a gun? A school shooting. What is the best thing about buying a gun? You get the most bang for your buck. What does a gun sound like in a church? *Pew pew pew.* What's the difference between a woman and a gun? You can put a silencer on a gun.

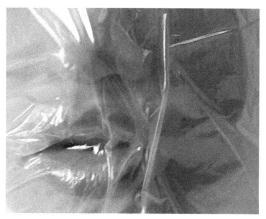

Chekhov says it's wrong to make promises

Bridget Kriner

you don't mean to keep, dear reader. Like when I
am weaving my way through a series of fine points,
and you watch me as I hang this gun with histrionic

subtlety on the wall of my writing studio, next to the tapestry
I barely mention, a landscape of some place
I never even been & you're a good sport, believing

I will fire. Otherwise, I shouldn't have described
the weight of cold danger, how the sleek industrial
track lights in my armory nook emphasize the woodsy

grain of the wall where I mount my guns, stitching each
into the tale, just in case I need one later. Though chances are,
clever reader, if it hangs, it will not even shoot, a mere set piece,

an unfireable symbol, or like Hemingway, maybe I am just queer
for guns. You can't be sure. & you know, he didn't even follow
his own rules—like if a broad comes

in the first scene, she must come again later. Just as in life,
hanging a gun without a plan is like going to the range
without bullets, but you know already, as a savvy reader,

how to decipher extraneous details, like how I always carry
a revolver, a throwaway piece of contrasting color I never
even touch, not a single pistol shot in the entire

yarn, but then I pick up my needles & cast on
again, knitting into the fabric, purling my way back,
gazing at an old chesnut-colored rifle with soft eyes.

There has to be a better way to die

Peter Crowley

I.

silver cells abound in glistening field
the body turns, a whooping crane listens.
Fish beneath the shadowed surface
dart in seizure spasms
The crane's beak jabs into the water, lacerating gills

II.

hairless, mouth ajar, dark circles underneath the eyes,
stomach in rebellion, T cells on strike.

There has to be a better way to die

listless, pallor, eyes fluttering, hallucinating,
blind, cancer in recession, it doesn't matter anymore.

There has to be a better way to die

feeding tubes, morphine, high fever, delirium,
tired like Vishnu imbibing all the world's suffering.

There has to be a better way to die

A Day at the Beach

Mary Paulson

Wordsworth organized the event.

But it was Simic who sat next to me most of the day,
pushing at the sand with his
fur-covered toes.

Blake made a brief appearance but
he seemed
distracted,
                confused,
and didn't want to sit down.

Anne Sexton lay like an Egyptian queen
        under the glare of orange sun—

long cigarette dangling from her fingers, black
one-piece encasing her tall figure,
her big, throaty laugh vibrating
through the arid August atmosphere—

All I remember about Sylvia is her clothes:
seersucker pants and a large sun hat.

                        *

The little boy with the group in front of us
whimpers, pulls at the seat
of his bathing suit, throws
his plastic sand shovel down, tears
twisting his baby face as he watches his brother
run off with the older boys

Child adversity—it hurts. Little
bones broken linger into adulthood become
        glass slivers, stabbing
fears, hopefully
he won't become a psychopath—

just the usual
        stress fractures—janky
rages, a twisty and incoherent
helplessness, excessive

hand washing, distorted
brain patterns, intimacy issues—

I feel for him but Charles and I agree,
in the long run, he'll be a more
interesting, nuanced
adult, in the
long run, he's better off.

Hours

Mary Paulson

a constant downpour is divine proof
       that everything is wrong, the way a sick body
is wrong, wrong—

inside, a thousand channels,
       a surreal, silver civilization
           biting into shadows meant for sleep—
unattended mail raises
       a pygmy-size mountain on the front, console table—

I'm here behind the window glass—
       a boundary that keeps the world
          on one side and me
          on the other
             but it's good this way—

I've heard there's a world of people who
       look like me, walk and talk
          like me but live life
          like it's a
             cozy house—

          life as a logical stream
       always in rhythm, as if
they hold nothing dear enough
          to fear for, while I've a feral monkey
           scrambling in my chest—

I know I don't help myself, watch
       too much TV, spend too much
          money online, crave and
          click, crave and click,
       I only lick my wounds when I'm alone—

       sleep is my cozy house, I
          dream, dream a life without
interminable evenings—

hours spent in misgiving,
in the uneasy marrow
of self-disgust,
the meaty, sleepless
blue dark.

Abracadabra

Antonia Alexandra Klimenko

> *Abracadabra*
> *a houseboat on the Canal Saint-Martin*

I cannot see you
but I know that you are there
like the sweet nostalgia of butterfly wings
the dust of memory between my fingers

Since you have gone my friend
all the ashtrays in Paris are full
all the bottles are empty
A thousand crows have flown
from your head into mine
clocks at the Musée D'Orsay
have decided to stand still
and Billie Holiday is beginning to sound
a lot like Leonard Cohen

I cannot see you
but I know that you are there
Two boats passing   between two dreams
drawing the sky's curtain between night and day
I walk with you   surreal   along the canal—
the winter moon drinking the river's dark

Since you have gone   my friend
since you and I have now   both decided
that *everyone* in Paris lives on the sixth floor
I wait for you at the top of my landing
I wait for you in small rooms with big hearts
I wait for you in all the stations of the soul
that have no last metro

I wait for you at stations
Saint-Germain and Saint-Michel

where   split in two   old friend
you look at me   I look at you

Your last night in Paris
still waves back to mine—
walk me to the corner,
*our steps will always rhyme**
Then   you turn the corner
as I turn this page

lyrics from Leonard Cohen's 1967 song, "Hey, That's No Way to Say Goodbye"

83.

Mystery Solved

Ron Kolm

My wife got home from work and our youngest son ran over to her and yanked her sleeve.

"Hey, Mommy, I saw Daddy on TV this afternoon," he shouted.

She had no idea what he was talking about, but she patted him on the head and told him to calm down.

I had left the house early and headed over to our local police precinct to pay a fine for accidentally adding some Styrofoam trays to our bag of recyclables. When I entered the station building, the desk sergeant looked up at me from his newspaper and broke into laughter.

"Yo, Joel Rifkin just wandered onto the premises!" he yelled into the rooms behind him. "He's probably looking for victim eighteen to fucking add to his total!"

A couple of uniformed cops charged into the room howling with glee.

"What can we do for ya, Joel-boy," the desk sergeant chortled.

When I got home that evening I told my wife what had occurred. We made a point of watching the news and the mystery got solved. I do look a lot like the serial killer. I shivered and turned away from the screen. She couldn't hide a smile, but so it goes.

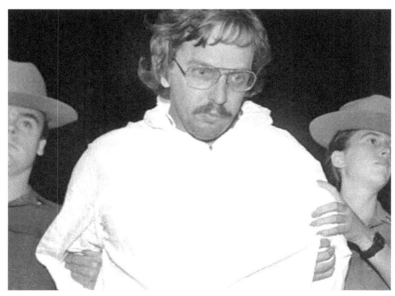

Extra Aloha Served Daily

Frankie Laufer

Some things are still sacred.
A giant green turtle passed by riding Duke's longboard.
A large wave at North Shore is standing on its hind legs and barking.
Even Uncle Kaai won't canoe here.
This water feels right even to those wearing slippers.
A shark swims close by but decides not to dine.
There is after all happy hour at Moana Surfrider later today.
Garlic shrimp at Giovanni's draws a mostly orderly crowd.
There are free hugs to everyone, even the haole in the I Heart NY hat.
Hawaii for Hawaiians flag flutters from a torn tent on Kahauiki.
Original spirit collides with million-dollar homes.
But damn, that blue ocean is mana from heaven.
Coffee, Mangoes, Papaya, Beautiful Women all have something in common, but I digress.
Enjoy what you can and leave the Aloha to the natives.

A Day at the Mall, Or: Gladiators' Cocktail Hour

Frankie Laufer

These people were mostly men dressed in green corn stalks.
Or was it seaweed? I'm not sure.
They rode roller coaster conveyor belts higher and higher in
search of food and a place to shelter.
I'm afraid of heights.
They temporarily adopted me and shared what appeared to be a secret
code.
Written in some unknown language on a piece of burlap.
But like a two-step login identification I didn't quite get it memorized
in time.
I was distracted by a rowdy group of Boy Scouts singing "Happy Birth-
day."
Huge blocks of garbage rolled by, tightly wrapped in tidy squares.
Everyone seemed okay, for now.
I believed them to be part of the mall teardown as the Prada signage
crashed to the nonexistent linoleum.
This felt like something much bigger was happening like a matrix of
sacred vortexes.
Everything was moving very quickly and blending like a mixer high on
speed.
Everyday people mingling with dreams from another place and time.
Hopes and desires looking for some consolation.
Among all this I spotted Maria who had just gotten off work.
She was walking in a parade of nicely dressed women.
Women I had loved or had wanted to love.
But not in this lifetime.
Venus in the twelfth house will do that.
We shared a sweet embrace, just like old times.
This feeling always travels well.
I will find her again, or maybe not.
I heard from her friend in the shiva yellow dress that she had another
baby.
His name is Frankie.
This makes me smile.

But I digress.

I located the mall entrance, or was it the Roman Colosseum?

Gladiators driving bulldozers had finally carved a way out of this maze.

This looked dangerous so I grabbed onto the chariot of steel and hung on.

Fortunately, I saw an old high school friend on a cruise who was helping with the luggage.

They extended a helping hand and added me to the carousel of floating bags.

Maria was tired and so was I.

Waking up now.

Shrove Tuesday

David Barnes

Pancake Day, as was,
in Mum's kitchen with the batter and the special flat pan.
Our pillow fights chased the dark outside and then
we took turns to pour planets and moons
tossed them over and over till we got it right,
heated up the jam.
That griddle could scare off ghosts—
we presented ourselves with our plates
and the priestcook shrove us
absolved us with sugar
and from winter set us free.

Next breakfast in America
bottomless mugs of coffee
and pancakes a half-inch thick:
sponges that soaked in syrup,
that tore under their own weight when lifted on the fork,
the crust crunchy-edged,
inside—pale bubbles like seed-spaces.
they were as big as your spread hand
and no Englishman could eat three.
In diners, Denny's and the Amtrak dining car
I ate them as the maple syrup darkened their interior
until there was just debris
a ruin of a pancake
dregs of sweetness and crumbs

Now these delicate doilies they call crêpes
thin as Parisians, thin as Lent,
I scrape the plate with my metal spoon
devour the lacework of fine holes.
All this feels like short shrift
and I say
Where is Fat Tuesday?

Ash Wednesday will arrive like a hangover,
like the aftermath of a sugar rush,
the gray dawn will filter through the windows,
touch its finger to your forehead to bring that dull ache that says
Remember you are dust
and to dust you shall return

*this poem originally appears in David Barnes' poetry collection, Poets Are Liars
Who Tell the Truth, available via Corrupt Press

Sunday Morning Market

David Barnes

By the dry fountain
we sat to eat
across from the fish stall.
The white-haired fishmother
packed away quicksilver sardines into polystyrene boxes.
Mackerel, smoked gold, lay on the table.
Water streamed off the corners from the melting ice.

We turned our knees towards each other,
our backs to the market eddying around us.
I put the paper cup of sauce on the worn bench
and we took nems, hot to the fingers,
from their grease-streaked paper bag.
The air was cold and bright,
you were in your thick coat
though it was not yet winter,
subdued.
We shared the crunchy sweetness.

The young men on the fruit and veg stall called to anyone in earshot,
generous with clementine segments, bunches of parsley.
Confident young men with an easy way and full of talk.
The world was a cousin they were welcoming back home.
Our granny trolley was crammed full.
Olive oil, walnuts, goat's cheese...
the dusty purple figs you enthused over,
the week's veg that we would stir-fry, steam, bake in the oven.
I watched you in your blue coat—
sticky fingers, sticky drops of sauce on the serviette
while people moved around us like the sea
and we sat on our island bench.
Reduced to the sensuality of sleep and tasty food,

you had slept through summer and were now getting ready to hibernate,
holding out for next year's thaw.
There was nothing to do.
It was a moment for sharing nems.

*this poem originally appears in David Barnes' *poetry collection,* Poets Are Liars
Who Tell the Truth, *available via Corrupt Press*

Owl

David Barnes

I saw the bird brains of my generation scattering in all directions, flocking homeless
      through the empty skies at dawn in search of an empty nest,
who sat up all night hollow-boned and high above the unnatural floating darkness of city
      streets, contemplating taxis and examinations and other things unprepared for,
who dove off roofs, off bridges, off tower blocks, squawking and fluttering uselessly all
      the way down, in a failed attempt to return to the egg
who hovered in universities, radiant with hawk-eyed visions of the next room, wider
      cages, sunlight on a far horizon of steel bars,
who sought the aviary, or a gilded cage, or always a higher perch, only to wind up
      confined with the other cuckoos, drained and dreary in the birdhouse of zoo,
who shat, delicately, along calculated shite-lines, on the targeted heads of commuters
      pouring out of metro tunnels, gravity-bound and beetle-black, a tide of humanity
      to which we would never belong,
who cheeped, cawed or sang to the dawn, great songs of joy when the world was
      empty, otherwise quiet, and the sleepers slept,
who swivel-necking and owl-eyed floated silently across fields of death, hunting without
      mercy the metaphorical unlucky mouse.

this poem originally appears in David Barnes' poetry collection, Poets Are Liars
Who Tell the Truth, *available via Corrupt Press*

The last time I saw my mother...

David Barnes

The last time I saw my mother
She was pushing me out of a moving taxi in Istanbul
She was setting off on a final ascent of the north face of Everest
She was being dragged screaming blue murder into the police van
She was cooking beef stew just the way we liked it
She was taking aim from the window of the Dallas book depository
She was giving her acceptance speech for the Nobel Peace Prize
She was running off with her tango instructor
She was cooking stew with human bone just the way we liked it
She was indoctrinating herself into her own religion, for tax purposes
She was wanted by the FBI
My mother; they don't make 'em like that anymore

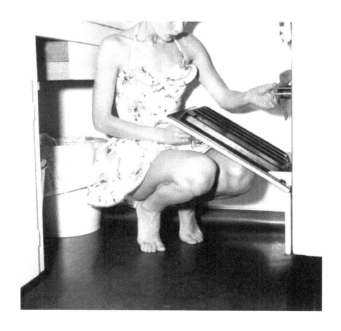

this poem originally appears in David Barnes' poetry collection, Poets Are Liars
Who Tell the Truth, *available via Corrupt Press*

I Am the Apeman, I Am Belarus

Charles March

To solemnly witness
                testicular
                 cancer
              is
to publicly   testify against
the
Declaration of   Independence's
      nudity.   After
             expressing
              its
objectionable
  balls
to avow
the   recusing
                wedding
     vows of a
   civics   professor,
submit an
       inhumane
       insurance
        claim   against
the   member's
       firm   asseverate
     with
      an
      argue
      fugue
      upon
the high
    sleep-in seas
         of
      mutinous
       boys

who sit
               on   disgusting
            cots
          in Obama
                barracks
         with   human
                    chains around
their   makeshift
                    Molotov
                     cocktail
                     necks,
                      just
before   walking
     off
     of
the   skanky
   political
   payout

                    plank
                     and
                    plunging
to
the
bottom
to
 occupy a wall street urchin
          as   a demonstration
       against the
      Illuminati's weather
                    controlling
                    lightning
    storm
    system   which
perpetuates
the colorful
    California   wildfires,
per
the
pirates'
   corporeal   rules,
because   it's

impossible
to tally
the
    rallies
        outside
        of
the   white
                    picket
                     fenced
                 ghettos
                        of
                 Jericho's
                 gherao,
even if   you
                    put
                 a   stoppage
to
the   anthrax
                    mail
                        art
                    stampage
                 containing
                    empty
                        promises
        of
    shooting
        blank   tears
        of   gas
                                 masturbation
    onto   a nuclear
                                 family
                                 fusion
                             immolation
                                 sit-in
    monk   playing
                                 a tie-die
                                 sitar
                                 getting

            raked over
the   coals
        as

the
field   tillers
that   enact
             policies
                 geared
                 toward
             atrocities
  get
their   fill
   at
the   altars
of   authoritarian
             aliens
who   spread
             culture
                     jamming
                     jelly on
the   bread
that   none
                     of
             us are baking.

Prey to the Undertow

Susan Richardson

The day I turned eight
you told me I came from the sea,
born on the beach
into the arms of a turbulent summer.
I sat quietly, listening,
as you embroidered the shape of my life,
words echoed by sea spray
as we ate roast beef sandwiches
and watched the waves attack the shore.
It was the first time I felt the sting of not fitting in,
the freak on my back,
sunlight trapped in my mouth.
You laughed and spread a blanket over the wind,
said I was special,
told me to hold on tightly to the corners.
Were you warning me
the tide would creep up and pull me in?

You sutured my emptiness
with stories of a twin who died at birth,
torn from your grasp by the rage of the current,
a tapestry of fiction
spun from the threads of your imagination
to make me feel unique and less alone.
You told me I was beautiful,
but it was a lie
constructed to paint the sun into a storm
that threatened to darken my eyes.
Did you know I would inherit your sorrow,
a lifetime of stitching up bones
to make myself solid,
only to get knocked down
by the murmurs of a spiteful mind?

The taste of that day lingers,
cloying and blistered on my tongue,

a tangle of images
you painted with flourish into the sand.
Your laughter was so vibrant
even the ocean couldn't swallow it.
Did you know then,
leaning softly against the backdrop of the sky,
that you would die ten years later,
leaving me prey to the undertow?

CRITICISM

Leave the World Behind's Film Version One-Ups the Novel With Small But Effective Additions— Including Amplifying the Use of Friends

Genna Rivieccio

It's a rare thing for a film adaptation to be able to truly surpass a book version of something. Perhaps the only known mainstream cases have been *The Shining*, *Legally Blonde* and *Mean Girls* (yes, you should know that the latter two were adapted from books). And yet, that's what Sam Esmail has managed to do with Rumaan Alam's 2020 novel, *Leave the World Behind*. Not just because he extracts the elements that are most cinematic—turning a one(ish)-location script into a near blockbuster—but because of the specific kernels from the book he chooses to extrapolate and transmogrify into an entire narrative thread. Not least of which is thirteen-year-old Rose's (Farrah Mackenzie) obsession, in the movie, with finding out how *Friends* will conclude. This becomes an increasingly remote possibility as she, her brother, Archie (Charlie Evans), and their parents, Amanda (Julia Roberts) and Clay (Ethan Hawke), realize that the internet is "down." That bizarre turn of phrase we use to indicate that there is no Wi-Fi. No connectivity. In other words, no fun. At least, that's what it means for most average Americans (of which there are many). Especially for the generation that has never experienced an existence without internet—Rose and Archie being just such poor souls. Though, of course, they would say

"As things start to become more glaringly chaotic by the time the Scotts show up, Amanda returns to her primal state of fear—the primordial trait within us all that keeps justifying the practice of othering—convinced that the man and woman who materialize at 'their' doorstep mean to do them harm. Or are somehow 'related' to all the 'weirdness' that's been going on."

it sounds like a nightmare to have ever lived without the internet when the reality is, the nightmare scenario comes from having a dependency on it once it invariably "goes down" (this being a long-standing fear of many who foresee it as the next version of a "Dark Age").

A dependency that has become so pervasive and deep-seated thanks to corporate and government abetment that it's almost like, hmmm, they *want* people to be dependent on it. And it's worked. Far too well, as Alam lays out in the novel. One in which Amanda and Clay embark on this vacation with what seems like slightly more preplanning than the Amanda and Clay of the film. Movie Amanda is the one who takes the initiative in booking this last-minute trip as an end-of-the-summer hurrah. A bid to get out of the city and the oppressive feeling it gives her (complete with Julia Roberts' now immortal line, "I fucking hate people").

Written just before the pandemic broke out, the novel's release occurred amid the unprecedented lockdowns/restrictions of Covid-19. As such, there is an uncanny reflection of "that life" and "those fears" present throughout the book. A tinge that is even more palpable in the film version, which, in contrast to the book, starts out with Amanda hurriedly getting ready for their trip to Long Island. One, it is made clear, that she booked on a whim because: "It's just been such a hellish year for us, as you know, and I just seem to be working every day without even realizing it. And you are just constantly anxious about your job because of all the budget cuts." Clay, still in bed half-asleep, tries to process where she's going with all of this when she gets to the point: "So I went online this morning and rented us a beautiful house out by the beach."

Alam, in lieu of this, simply starts the book out with the Sandfords in the car, en route to the "removed" location in question. And it's a car described as "a middle-class thing for middle-class people, engineered not to offend more than to appeal..." This detail immediately telling of the Sandfords' wish to just, for one week, pretend to live slightly above their station. Such a prosaic desire is additionally expressed when Alam writes, "Clay had tenure, and Amanda had the title of director, but they did not have level floors and central air-conditioning. The key to success was having parents who had succeeded. Still, they could pantomime ownership for a week." Or so they thought they could...

Among the details that do not occur in the car of the book is Rose watching *Friends* (how middle class indeed). Specifically, episode eleven of season ten: "The One Where the Stripper Cries." Which automatically indicates she's approaching the final episode of the series, "The Last One." A bittersweet reality that she, like many viewers before her, must endure in order to join the millions of others who have seen the show through like a badge of honor. Later on, a certain character in *Leave the World Behind* will express how very sad that makes you as a person to feel such a way about *Friends*. But in the meantime, no derisive commentary is made about the show and its overtly problematic nature.

It is perhaps this particular adaptation decision on Esmail's part that makes the film so uniquely superior to the book. Even though the latter does mention the series in a rather offhanded manner...all the way on the second to last page. But, obviously, it is not interwoven throughout the entire narrative the way it is in the film version. Her discovery of the *Friends* DVD box sets in the book transpires when Rose returns to the house she previously saw from her vantage point in the woods. Unlike in the movie, it isn't a "bunker" she finds, but an ordinary abode. One that she explores with interest, eventually returning to "the den and switch[ing] on the television. The screen was blue. Rose opened the cabinet beneath it and found the PlayStation, the dozens of plastic boxes holding the various games, and dozens of DVDs. They didn't have a player at their house, but there was one in the classroom, and she was not stupid. She decided on *Friends*; they had the whole box set. It was the episode where Ross fantasized about Princess Leia." Better known as "The One With the Princess Leia Fantasy." But sticking with this premiere episode from season three wouldn't behoove the sense of urgency Rose has about finishing the series. Already being midway through season ten, she absolutely *has to* finish it. *Has to* know what happens, how it ends.

There are other noticeable "Esmail stamps" on everything, including the dialogue. Not to mention the addition of some very specific scenes. For example, at the Charleston Harbor Beach (as fictional as the "Point Comfort" town where they're staying on Long Island), the family's idyllic day is "rudely" interrupted when an oil tanker inexplicably heads straight for the shore. A harbinger that, at last, can't be ignored (or so one would think). Though, at first, Amanda is thrilled to remark, "We practically have the beach to ourselves," the running theme of *Leave the World Behind* is that, while misanthropes despise other people in theory, when they're all actually gone and out of sight, the implications become a little too real. Those "few" people on the beach who have the luxury of continuing not to notice that something very "off" is happening back in "mainland" civilization are part of Esmail's commentary on privilege. How it insulates certain people for so much longer than others from the inevitable fallout of "fucking with Nature." Or, in this case, failing to realize that, sooner or later, someone would think to cause an insurrection (far more successful than the one attempted on January 6th) via the mass panic of "taking down" the internet. The probability of which might not be as likely as *Leave the World Behind* makes it seem when taking into account that fiber optic cables are still the crux of the internet's functionality as opposed to satellite and other wireless communications.

When the man ushering the beachgoers back to their cars tells Clay, "There's been a handful of these groundings up the coast. Something to do with the nav system," it comes across as even more absurd that so many people are ignoring the very alarming signs right in front of them (making this, yet again, eerily prescient and aligned with the year 2020). "Turning a blind eye" whenever possible despite knowing the dangers of random oil tanker groundings, no one thought to perhaps close the beaches or put out warning signs. No one, after all, wants to be "alarmist" about anything, lest it affect the financial bottom line by preventing people from going out and spending (hence, the mayor in *Jaws* also refusing to properly warn beachgoers about a certain danger). What's more, people—even those, like Amanda and Clay, who view themselves as far more intelligent than the average—are only too happy to help play into the delusion that "everything is fine." That it takes the oil tanker nearly crashing right into their umbrella for the family to start believing Rose after she already warned them about it from the outset is yet another sign of the human inability to believe what they see right in front of them. This has only amplified in the internet age, with many convinced that everything is a fabrication or embellishment at this point—even when they see something incontrovertible with their own eyes. This, in part, is why most are prone to filming a horrific or traumatic event (just as Archie films the massive tanker while they're running for their lives from it). They need to play it back later to ensure what they saw was real.

Despite the unsettling beach outing, both Archie and Rose appear to recover quickly back at the house, swimming in the luxurious pool as though nothing odd at all just happened. A recovery so quick, in fact, that Amanda comments, "The kids seem to have completely gotten over it, like it was something they saw on a show. They're on to the next episode." (This being a signature piece of added "Esmail dialogue" not present in the book.) Her undercutting condemnation of Gen Z apathy aside, it's not as though she herself didn't recover quickly on the way back when she gleefully pointed out a Starbucks she wanted to pop into. For people—nay, Americans—are always capable of remaining calm so long as they can keep returning to the comforts of capitalism. That's how they can tell that nothing cataclysmic has *really* happened. Reassured by a place like Starbucks continuing to be open—even in the face of calamity—that nothing can be *too* wrong with the world.

Obviously, though, there is. But the Sandfords are too willfully oblivious to accept it in spite of so many portents. Not just the massive oil tanker and the mention of its faulty nav system, but the fact that the Wi-Fi isn't working, their phones have no service and the TV is only showing static for a suspicious amount of time. Instead, they choose to see the arrival of the Scotts as the "bad omen." And yeah, it's undoubtedly a result of the Scotts being Black—though Amanda is the one who displays her racism about their "infiltration" the most overtly.

In the book, Alam highlights the internal war between her "noble white womanhood" and her, for lack of a better term, "Karenness." The latter quality prompting a small description about Amanda's co-worker, Jocelyn, that allows Alam to explain her hypocrisy in one fell swoop: "Jocelyn, of Korean parentage, had been born in South Carolina, and Amanda continued to feel that the woman's mealymouthed accent was incongruous. This was so racist she could never admit it to anyone." Because, on the outside, she's supposed to present as a "good" and "kind" human being. But, as Amanda points out several times throughout the film, these are two characteristics that actually go entirely against human nature (William Golding knew that).

As things start to become more glaringly chaotic by the time the Scotts show up, Amanda returns to her primal state of fear—the primordial trait within us all that keeps justifying the practice of othering—convinced that the man and woman who materialize at "their" doorstep mean to do them harm. Or are somehow "related" to all the "weirdness" that's been going on. G.H. (Mahershala Ali), now a much suaver, younger man than the one in the book, does his best to put her at ease, even making the Luddite comment, "This is why I much preferred life before the internet. Because we would have spoken over the phone, you would have recognized my voice and known that this is our house." As for Ruth (Myha'la), who has, for the purposes of this movie, been transformed into G.H.'s daughter instead of remaining his wife, she runs out of patience with Amanda's boiling-to-the-surface racism far sooner. Arguably from the moment Amanda essentially looks them (and their Blackness) up and down with skepticism before saying, "This is *your* house?" They're then "permitted" entry so that G.H. can give further explanation, including the mention of how their phones didn't have service to call beforehand. When Amanda replies that her phone doesn't have service either, Ruth ripostes, "It's almost as if we're telling the truth."

As usual, though, people find it all but impossible to take the truth at face value—constantly trying to poke holes in it to unearth an "explanation" that makes more sense to them. A narrative that's more "palatable." This is why it takes Amanda and Clay such a long time to fully accept what has happened. And, by the same token, such a long time for Rose to accept that she won't ever be able to stream *Friends* again. Because, unfortunately, the internet makes the world go 'round. Extending most notably into the entertainment sphere. Or, to be more accurate, the "keeping them entertained" sphere. Because without the distraction of internet-based media, the masses definitely do become "less controllable" (read: less prone to total oblivion). As the internet-dependent have learned in the past, there can sometimes be a price to pay for being so addicted to entertainment delivered through this medium.

With Esmail being "Mr. Robot" himself, it's no surprise that he inserts dialogue for G.H. to recite that makes mention of the infamous 2000 "Love Bug," one of the most well-known computer viruses to wreak havoc on a mass scale even to this day. G.H. wants to believe it's

"People find it all but impossible to take the truth at face value—constantly trying to poke holes in it to unearth an 'explanation' that makes more sense to them. A narrative that's more 'palatable.' This is why it takes Amanda and Clay such a long time to fully accept what has happened. And, by the same token, such a long time for Rose to accept that she won't ever be able to stream *Friends* again."

something as innocuous as "two teenagers in the Philippines" fucking around, but, deep down, he knows better. As a financial analyst, the pattern he noticed just before this inexplicable and disturbing turn of events was enough for him to realize he should retreat to his remote house rather than remain in the already inherently chaotic city. In Book Ruth's opinion, "The city was as unnatural as it was possible to be, accretion of steel and glass and capital, and light was fundamental to its existence. A city without power was like a flightless bird, an accident of evolution." And that's exactly what it becomes in the wake of a terror attack that any number of America-hating countries could be responsible for. Though, the more likely scenario is that whoever is really behind it merely wants the masses to *believe* that a country like Iran or North Korea is the culprit. Ergo, leaflets dropped from the sky across the U.S.

in different languages. Korean, Arabic—depends on the location. But the point of the "exercise" is clearly to confuse everyone about what the fuck is actually happening and who's behind it. This, G.H. tells Clay, is "the most cost-effective way to destabilize a country." A "simple three-stage maneuver that could topple a country's government from within." With the simple act of disabling all communication systems by disabling the internet.

Part of that "synchronized chaos" G.H. talks about is best evinced by a scene Esmail adds into the film where it didn't exist in the book. Namely, he presents the Sandfords with the unexpected danger of the malfunctioning Teslas causing a massive roadblock in front of them as they foolishly try to return to the city. This scene, of course, provides the catalyst for why they end up returning to the Scotts' house after making a huge to-do about leaving and attempting to "go it alone." Such a selfish act, indeed, is the crux of *Leave the World Behind*'s theme, which posits there are two kinds of people when the shit hits the fan: those who want to "take care of their own" in a crisis and those who want to band together in the community they're with to better tackle the chaos as it comes. At first, Amanda seems to be a member of the former camp, until we see her start to warm to G.H. and Ruth. Even when Ruth derides her daughter's *Friends* obsession after seeing a scene from it frozen on the iPad because of the internet fuckery. She asks, "Your daughter watches that show?" Amanda answers, "'Watch' is far too weak of a word. More like worships." "Hmm." "What?" Ruth then explains, "Don't get me wrong, I watched it too. But it's almost nostalgic for a time that never existed, you know?" A time when, supposedly, friendship cabals could sub in for communities and families. Get each other through the bad times and the good (hence, "I'll be there for you/ When the rain starts to pour/I'll be there for you/Like I've been there before/I'll be there for you/'Cause you're there for me too").

In reality, it has always been as Amanda says it is during a frustrated soliloquy delivered in front of Ruth: "We fuck each other over all the time, without even realizing it. We fuck every living thing on this planet over and think it'll be fine because we use paper straws and order free-range chicken. And the sick thing is, I think deep down we know we're not fooling anyone. I think we know we're living a lie. An agreed-upon mass delusion to help us ignore and keep ignoring how awful we really are." In the book version, Alam writes that as: "People kept calling the Amazon the planet's lungs. Waist-deep water was lapping against Venetian marble, and tourists were smiling and taking snapshots. It was like some tacit agreement; everyone had ceded to things just falling apart. That it was common knowledge that things were bad surely meant they were actually worse."

Yet who needs (or wants) to truly address just how much worse when they have a numbing agent like *Friends*? An "antidote," as it were, for reality. Causing Rose to "use" guilt-free because media consumption is arguably the most acceptable form of drug abuse. Thus, at the beginning of the film, Rose's multi-pronged obsession with the show manifests further when she inquires, "Dad, when we get back to the city, can you take me to see the coffee shop in *Friends*?" Clay reminds, "I don't think that's real, honey. It's, uh, just a set." Something that, of course, should be fairly obvious. Even to the untrained eye. But her refusal to believe that nothing about *Friends* is genuine plays into the aforementioned inability of people to trust what's actually real versus placing all their faith in the fake. After asking that question, "Misled" by Kool & the Gang fittingly plays over the next scene, with lyrics that forewarn of something ominous as Robert "Kool" Bell sings, "What's this crazy place, you want to take me to?/Tell me, what's the price if I go with you?" Elsewhere, he demands, "Won't you be for real?" (Needless to say, Esmail's musical choices are also paramount to the reason why the film ends up making a greater impact.) But that's an impossible task for most people in this epoch, one in which they've all been forced to become, in one way or another, ersatz. An avatar of themselves. Making it difficult to distinguish between what's real and what's not anymore. And, what most people have forgotten about altogether is the realest thing of all: Mother Nature. Anyone jadedly scoffing about how we need to "go back to the soil" would be easily put into their place with a single catastrophic event like the one that happens in *Leave the World Behind*. Though there are still a lot of people who don't see "losing" the internet as a catastrophe so much as a blessing, there's no denying how fucked most of us would be without it at this juncture. Our collective dependency on it enabled by the government and big business for so long that we can almost accuse them of being Sackler-esque.

In the novel, Alam conveys this type of dependency and its eventual fallout as follows: "All it took to unravel something was one party deciding to do just that. There was no real structure to prevent chaos, there was only a collective faith in order." This, through Esmail's own writerly interpretation, becomes: "A conspiracy theory about a shadowy group of people running the world is far too lazy of an explanation. Especially when the truth is much scarier... No one is in control. No one is pulling the strings... When events like this happen in the world, the best [that] even the most powerful people can hope for is a heads up."

The implication in both narratives is that the only way to rebuild after an inevitable mass breakdown of "civilization" as we know it is through small communities. Even if comprised of those one wouldn't ordinarily "gravitate toward" by choice. Instead, the coming together of people would likely arise in the same way it does for the Sandfords and the Scotts: out of necessity and having no other real options. Rose, however, does find herself an option in the rich people's bunker she happens upon. One that is filled with essential rich people fixings (e.g., top-of-the-line exercise equipment, varied meal choices in the pantry and a computer setup that can tell what the radiation levels are outside). In other words, not your mother's bomb shelter. Rose doesn't appear all that fazed by the idea that she might have to hole up inside this place for the foreseeable future. Not once she sees that the shelter is equipped with every season of *Friends* on DVD. At last, she can watch the final episode...sans having to bother with watching the world burn at all. It's not as though she (and everyone else) wasn't already doing the same thing before while still passively standing (or, rather, sitting) by anyway. Now that's it's actually burned, there's even more guiltlessness to the numbing out. What Alam elucidates by remarking of Rose's discovery, "The sound of the television made her feel so much better. She turned the volume loud to keep her company as she ransacked."

This is a far cry from her former worried state in the film as she asks Archie, "I'm never going to find out what happens to Ross and Rachel am I?" Amazed that such a concern could be her primary one amidst everything that's happening, Archie snaps, "You're still on this shit? Who gives a fuck?" Rose answers, "Well I do, obviously." Archie, genuinely wanting to comprehend her fixation, says, "Why do you care so much about that show anyway?" Rose, with a totally serious expression on her face, explains, "They make me happy. I really need that right now. Don't you?... If there's any hope left in this fucked-up world, I wanna at least find out how things turn out for them. I care about them." Archie seems to wish he hadn't asked, because it only makes her sound all the more pathetic to him.

Nonetheless, this notion of "needing" to know how something ends in a movie or TV series is a larger symptom of needing to know how things will end for humanity. For the constant sense of impending doom these past several years has led to a collective obsession with wanting to know not *if* it's all going to end, but *when*. Because knowing when would surely affect the amount of effort people kept putting into the game of capitalism—complete with bothering to waste what precious hours are left on working an unfulfilling job.

To this point, though, Alam carefully chooses his final words for *Leave the World Behind* to speak to that evermore omnipresent human concern: "If they didn't know how it would end—with night, with more terrible noise from the top of Olympus, with bombs, with disease, with blood, with happiness, with deer or something else watching them from the darkened woods—well, wasn't that true of every day?" Why, yes, come to think of it, it is. Even so, this conclusion is not nearly as satisfying as being able to get to see Rose fulfill her superficial dream of finishing *Friends*. Maybe because it's an only too accurate reflection of how all our own superficial dreams get us through the sky falling on a day-to-day basis.

If you like The Opiate magazine, you'll love The Opiate Books. Find our current roster of titles (featured below) online or at your favorite bookstore. Visit theopiatemagazine.com for more information.

Brontosaurus Illustrated
by Leanne Grabel
Released: June 2022
List price: $34.99

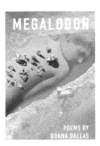

Megalodon
by Donna Dallas
Released: April 2023
List price: $10.99

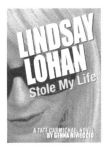

Lindsay Lohan Stole My Life
(A Tate Carmichael Novel)
by Genna Rivieccio
Released: April 2023
List price: $18.99

The PornME Trinity
(2nd Edition)
by David Leo Rice
Released: October 2022
List price: $12.99

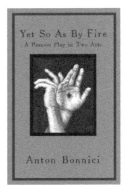

Yet So As By Fire: A Passion Play in Two Acts
by Anton Bonnici
Released: December 2021
List price: $10.99

Quasar Love: A Reenactment in Three Acts
by Anton Bonnici
Released: August 2022
List price: $10.99

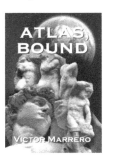

Atlas, Bound
by Victor Marrero
Released: July 2023
List price: $15.99

I Love Paris
by Rufo Quintavalle
Released: September 2023
List price: $10.99

Milton Keynes UK
Ingram Content Group UK Ltd.
UKHW051104190224
438087UK00007B/99